She'd know him anywhere.

The way he stood against the truck. The way he pushed his cowboy hat back. After all these years Rem was still familiar to her. Her heart did a flip she had to ignore.

"What are you doing here?" she asked.

"I was driving through town and I saw you running. I didn't want to leave you here alone."

"I'm a big girl. No one needs to rescue me."

The words slipped out. Not that he would understand what they meant. He wouldn't guess that she'd waited for exactly that ten years ago. That summer she'd learned a lesson about love and everything it wasn't.

"Samantha, I'm sorry they sent you away." His voice mixed with a coyote's howl and a train whistle. The night sounds of Martin's Crossing.

"Me, too." She opened her mouth to tell him more but she couldn't. Not yet.

Maybe everyone had been right. What they'd had was nothing more than a teen crush. A mistake.

But when she looked at him, an insistent thought echoed in her mind. *Was it?*

Brenda Minton lives in the Ozarks with her husband, children, cats, dogs and strays. She is a pastor's wife, Sunday school teacher, coffee addict and sleep-deprived. Not in that order. Her dream to be an author for Harlequin started somewhere in the pages of a romance novel about a young American woman stranded in a Spanish castle. Her dreams came true, and twenty-plus books later, she is an author hoping to inspire young girls to dream.

Books by Brenda Minton

Love Inspired

Martin's Crossing

A Rancher for Christmas
The Rancher Takes a Bride
The Rancher's Second Chance
The Rancher's First Love

Lone Star Cowboy League

A Reunion for the Rancher

Cooper Creek

Christmas Gifts
"Her Christmas Cowboy"
The Cowboy's Holiday Blessing
The Bull Rider's Baby
The Rancher's Secret Wife
The Cowboy's Healing Ways
The Cowboy Lawman
The Cowboy's Christmas Courtship
The Cowboy's Reunited Family

Visit the Author Profile page at Harlequin.com for more titles.

The Rancher's First Love

Brenda Minton

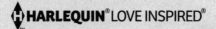

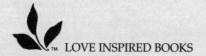

LOVE INSPIRED BOOKS

Recycling programs
for this product may
not exist in your area.

ISBN-13: 978-0-373-71940-2

The Rancher's First Love

Copyright © 2016 by Brenda Minton

www.Harlequin.com

Printed in U.S.A.

Unfailing love and truth have met together.
Righteousness and peace have kissed!
—*Psalms* 85:10

To great friends who keep me going.
Yeah, you know your names.
Love you all to the moon and back. And to
Melissa Endlich, editor supreme. Your patience
and wisdom are appreciated beyond belief.

Chapter One

The pediatric rehab wing of the Braswell, Texas, Doctor's Hospital sounded like an out-of-control playground when Samantha Martin walked through the double doors. A little boy in a wheelchair zoomed her way, his face split in a wide grin.

"You're here," he announced.

"Of course I'm here, Parker. I work here." She took the handles of the wheelchair and pushed him back down the hall. "Why are you racing around like a maniac?"

"The cowboys are coming today."

"Cowboys?" Three days off and she no longer knew what was going on. She did know that after being outside in the June sunshine, the air-conditioning felt good and the kids all seemed to have spring fever. "Are we having a rodeo on the unit? Or football?"

She glanced at one of the other nurses. The woman shrugged as she headed into a room with a toddler on her hip. The Braswell hospital, just a short distance from Samantha's home in Martin's Crossing, was small but efficient. And the staff cared. It was a great place to begin her career as an RN.

At the moment she didn't have a lot of time to reflect on her job, not with Parker, a dark-haired rascal, talking ninety miles an hour. She must have missed half of what the little boy said because he was glancing back at her as if she didn't have a clue.

"I'm sorry, Parker. So…cowboys are coming today. "

"One of them is my cousin. And they're bringing a real, live horse!"

That got her attention. "They can't bring a horse into the hospital."

An aid stuck her head out of the door to the room next to Parker's. "Miniature horse. It's approved."

Seriously? "Okay, they're bringing a horse. That should be interesting."

"You think it'll go to the bathroom, don't you?" Parker asked.

"Well, it is a horse. They aren't typically house-trained." She lifted him from his chair and placed him in bed. "Stay."

"I got myself out earlier."

She gave him a serious look. "Not without supervision, buddy."

The nine-year-old nodded. "Okay, not without supervision. But Danny was in here."

"Danny is ten. He doesn't count."

She gave him one last warning look and headed back to the nurse's station. "We have to move Parker closer to the nurse's station. He escaped his bed again."

"You can't stop determination." Dr. Jackson grinned as he entered something in the computer. He was older and liked to remind them he'd seen it all.

"No, but I can stop him from falling and getting hurt."

"Good luck," the doctor said as he pulled on glasses and meandered back down the hall. He said after thirty years of practicing, he no longer got too excited about anything.

But nurses did. That was their job. And right about now, all the nurses seemed a little too excited. It must have something to do with cowboys. If they'd grown up with her brothers, they wouldn't be excited about a bunch of domineering, take-charge men in chaps.

"So what are the cowboys doing here today?" she asked as she picked up a chart.

"Rope tricks, the pony of course and just looking pretty stinking good," Laura Struthers said, her voice ending on a whisper as she looked past Sam toward the door. "Wow. Those are some cowboys. Not the stinky, been-on-the-range-too-long kind, but the dressed-up, rugged, could-be-in-a-commercial kind."

"No thanks." Sam studied the chart. "I need to get Patricia down to X-Ray."

"Doc said not until after the cowboys."

"She needs…"

"Doc said."

"Fine," Sam caved. "I guess we won't do anything until the cowboys leave. But I'm going to check on Parker and make sure he's still in his bed."

She headed down the hall, back to Parker's room. When she stepped in, she froze. Not because of the miniature horse the boy was petting, but because of the cowboy standing at his side. There was something about the man standing next to the little boy's bed. It was in his build, in the way he stood, controlled yet relaxed. It was his dark hair, the hand that rested on the boy's arm and the way her traitor heart reacted, even without seeing his face.

"Your granny says they're letting you out of here real soon." The cowboy spoke in a low voice that vibrated through Sam.

"Yeah. And we're moving to Martin's Crossing." That was news to Sam, but she couldn't dwell on it. She had to escape. She backed away from the door.

"Nurse Sam!" Parker yelled.

She stopped in the doorway and peeked back into the room. The cowboy at Parker's side had turned. It was him. Remington Jenkins in the flesh. And none too happy to see her. The feeling was mutual.

But Parker had his blue eyes pinned on her and she had to respond. "Yes, Parker?"

"This is my cousin. He's a cowboy. I told you he was."

"Yes, you did tell me. And your cousin brought a pony to the hospital," she accused.

"He's housebroke," that same low, husky voice replied. She moved her gaze from the little black horse that came just above his knees to his face. His very familiar face.

At seventeen he'd been the cutest thing she'd ever seen. At twenty-seven he proved that age could be a good thing. Drat the man for his steel-gray eyes in a suntanned face, dark hair and five-o'clock shadow that covered the smooth planes of his face.

She swallowed. "Hi, Remington."

"Sam, it's been a long time."

Yes, it had. He'd never rescued her the way she'd dreamed he would do when her brothers had sent her away. She'd pictured him arriving in his old truck, radio blaring. He'd open the door, she'd jump in and in her sixteen-year-old mind they'd drive off into the sunset, broke and homeless but happy.

He hadn't even written.

"I didn't know you worked here. Parker has talked about his favorite nurse at rehab, but I had no idea she would be my favorite nurse, too." He gave her that easy, familiar smile of his, as if the past didn't exist. Maybe for him it didn't. Maybe walking away had been easy for Remington Jenkins.

He wasn't the first person who had no problem walking away from her.

She breathed through the pain and managed what she hoped was a carefree look. For Parker's sake, not his. "Yes, well, I have to get back to work. It was good seeing you."

It took everything in her to ignore the questions in Remington's eyes. It took more to ignore the questions in her heart. Why now? When she'd come home and rebuilt her life, why was he here now?

She hurried down the hall to the sanctuary of a linen closet. Inside that quiet space she closed the door and leaned her back against it. Alone and safe with her emotions, she closed her eyes and cried. She cried for little boys who would never walk again. She cried for everything she'd lost. Everything that ached inside her came out in hot, angry tears.

John Wayne followed Remington room to room. The tiny horse nuzzled children, sniffing their hands, closing his eyes and resting his head on their laps when they stroked his face and neck. John was a prize horse when it came to cheering up children. Remington had used him as a part of ministry for the past two years.

The little horse would also serve as their victim when it came time to show the kids some trick roping. John Wayne knew a few tricks. He'd even learned to "play like a calf" when roped. He would drop to the ground and let the guys tie his hooves. He also prayed when asked. He would extend his front legs and drop his head to the ground. Kids loved a praying horse. So did most adults.

Focusing on the horse and the kids helped Remington to ignore the obvious distraction of Sammy Martin. After all this time she still had the ability to undo his common sense. Her blond hair was a little shorter than it had been, but her blue eyes were just as blue and that pretty mouth… He smiled. How could a guy not remember strawberry lip gloss?

Her dad had died about the time he'd gone to work at the Martin ranch. It hadn't been a good time for the Martins. It hadn't been the best chunk of his own life, either.

He led John Wayne out of the room of a little girl who didn't speak. She reached one tiny hand to touch John. At least she'd reacted. Dr. Jackson told him that was probably a small miracle in itself. He liked the doctor who had made this unit a possibility. The hospital, typical for small communities, had few patients. This children's unit met a need and kept the hospital solvent. Most important, it gave hope.

The rest of his cowboy crew waited in the activity area for him to make his rounds. The kids were being moved to that area as he led John down the hallway. He looked up, meeting the brief accusing gaze of Samantha Martin. Those blue eyes could sure shoot sparks at a man. He wondered if she ever thought that he might have a little bit of a reason to be upset, too.

No, she probably didn't. She was a Martin. Her brothers, all three of them, had egos the size of the Rockies. Her older sister had been decent. A couple of years back Elizabeth and her husband had been killed in a small plane crash, leaving behind twin daughters. He knew from local gossip that Jake Martin was raising those little girls.

Jake, Duke, Brody, the three of them had caught him in the barn with Sam. He let go of the memory and met her gaze again. She looked away but not before he saw that her eyes were rimmed with red and her nose had turned pink. A sure sign she'd been crying.

Over him? Or was that just his ego talking? Working at the hospital as she did, he could see dozens of reasons she might cry from time to time.

He knew there were going to be problems with moving back to Martin's Crossing. Sam was one of them. Fortunately he didn't have time to focus on her or what she felt about him. He had his granddad to worry about. Gus wasn't doing too great. And now he had to think about Parker, too.

Sam moved past him, helping a little girl who made slow progress on crutches. She spoke softly, giving the child advice and encouragement. He couldn't help but notice her. The softness of her voice. The pink of her nails as she steadied the little girl. The scent of her, soft and floral.

Man, she smelled good.

A guy couldn't not notice when a woman smelled that good. Or when her blond hair shimmered beneath the lights. A man couldn't help notice blue eyes flecked with violet. Noticing was what had gotten him in trouble ten years ago.

He shook it off as John Wayne nipped at his jeans. "Hey, mule, stop that."

The little girl with Sam laughed. "He's not a mule. He's a pony."

He squatted in front of John and the little girl stopped, forcing Sam to stop. "He's actually a miniature horse."

"Why?" the child asked. Her big brown eyes moved from his face to the horse at his side. John lipped the hand she extended. He saved his teeth for Remington.

"That's a good question," he responded. "Ponies are breeds that stay under a certain size. Miniature horses are horses that just stay tiny."

She wrinkled her nose and shook her head. He looked up at Sam. She was giving him the same look.

"Not a good answer?" he asked. They both shook their heads and he laughed. "Yeah, it doesn't make a lot of sense to me, either. I just know that John Wayne here is a real good horse. And if we go in with the others, he'll show you some pretty amazing tricks."

He straightened, still holding the lead to John Wayne. The horse pulled him on in to the activity room, following behind temptation in nurse's scrubs. Pink scrubs with teddy bears.

For the next hour he entertained the children. He showed a little boy named Danny, an amputee, how to lasso John Wayne. They had a contest to see who could draw the best horse picture. Afterward, John did a few tricks. He played calf, prayed and climbed up on a pedestal, where he shook hands with various kids.

At the end of the program, Remington prayed. When he asked the children if they had any prayer requests, hands went up all over the room. He took out a pen and paper to write them all down. Nothing hurt a kid more than forgetting their request. It might be a prayer for a goldfish that died, but it still mattered. He wrote them all down and ignored the way Samantha Martin tried to avoid looking at him the entire time.

He had hoped that they could live in the same area and not bump into each other. It was a foolish hope. Since they were obviously going to see each other from time to time, he guessed they were going to have to talk.

But first he'd talk to God. He had a whole list of prayer requests from the kids, running the gamut from wanting a pony to being able to walk again. Kids always broke his heart. He never left one of these events without shedding a few tears.

It was something his granddad had taught him. Real men could cry.

After he'd prayed, he and the other guys went around the room, shaking hands and signing autographs. He'd brought some champions with him today. A Bull Riding World Champion, an All-Around Cowboy World Champion, a Steer Wrestling Champion and an award-winning stock contractor. They all had stories to share, roping tricks to display and pictures to hand out.

One of Remington's personal favorites was Bryan Cooper, from Dawson, Oklahoma. He'd met the younger man at a church event in Austin. Bryan had lived in South America and told a compelling story of forgiveness. For the children in these units, he talked about his faith as a young man.

As the cowboys circulated, Remington let his gaze

slide to the far wall. Samantha Martin stood to one side, watching him but pretending not to. He caught and held her gaze, because he enjoyed watching that flush of pink in her cheeks. She looked away first.

He squatted in front of a little girl in a wheelchair.

"Can I pet him?" she asked, pointing to John Wayne. Her voice was raspy and she closed her eyes as if talking hurt.

"You sure can." He pulled John a little closer. The girl reached out, tentative, stroking the soft muzzle of the horse.

"I used to have a pony," she said, not looking at him but her big brown eyes gobbling up his horse.

"Did you?"

She nodded. "Yeah, before. Before the fire."

Yeah, he was going to cry today. He could feel it coming on as the little girl told him about a fire and how her daddy got her out but then went back in for the rest of the family. And he didn't come back out again.

What did a man say to that? He wanted to tell this child he would fix it all. But he couldn't. He couldn't fix her. He couldn't give her back her family. So he hugged her and told her he would pray.

She leaned in close. "Pray someone wants to be my family."

His throat tightened painfully at that request. "You've got it, kiddo."

"My name is Lizzy," she whispered.

Samantha rescued him. She appeared at his side and as he stayed on his knees in front of Lizzy, she touched his shoulder.

"Time for lunch, Lizzy Lou." Sam brushed a hand

through the child's blond hair. "Tell Mr. Jenkins thank you."

"Thank you." Lizzy smiled sweetly. "I hope you'll come back soon."

"I sure hope I can, Lizzy." He stood and moved out of the way with John. "Maybe just John Wayne and me, but we'll be back."

"Don't make promises," Sam whispered as she walked away.

He couldn't let that go. He led John back to the nurse's station. He waited for Sam to walk back into the hall and he followed her.

"Go away, Rem." She spoke without looking back at him.

He caught up with her, tugging John along behind him. The pony trotted, but he pulled his head back, not happy with the pace.

"No, I don't think I will."

She spun to face him, her blue eyes flashing sparks of anger that would have quelled a lesser man. He reckoned she ought to know he wasn't going to be pushed around.

"Your posse left. Why didn't you leave with them?" she asked.

"Because it seems as if we have unfinished business."

She shook her head. "No, we don't. We've been finished for a long time now. We were kids, Rem. We're adults now and I don't have time for this."

"Why did you tell me not to make promises to that little girl?"

"Is that what this is all about?" She pulled a face at him, wrinkling her nose. "These kids have enough to deal with, and they don't need a cowboy and his pony trotting into their lives, cheering them up, and then promising to come back."

"But I *am* coming back. I've already talked to Dr. Jackson. I'm going to stop by every couple of weeks."

"Great," she said, not really meaning it. He half smiled, which would probably get him in more trouble.

"I made the offer before I knew you worked here. But surprise! I keep promises and I'm not going to back out on kids just because you don't want me here."

"It isn't about me."

He leaned in close. "Isn't it?"

She shook her head and put a little space between them. "No, it isn't. I just don't want these kids hurt or disappointed."

Hurt and disappointed. He knew right away that it *was* about her. But he wouldn't push and make her admit it. She'd just have to get used to having him around.

Chapter Two

The sun had long since set as Samantha drove through Martin's Crossing after work. She could go home to her house on the Circle M, have a sandwich, go to bed and not sleep. Or she could take a run and calm her mind. She pulled into an empty parking space in front of her brother Duke's diner. Duke's No Bar and Grill was a long wood-sided building with a wide, covered deck running the entire length of the front.

She got out of her truck, leaving the keys in the ignition. After all, this was Martin's Crossing; no one ever took the keys out of their ignition.

Sometimes they did. If there was a theft in the area, people might be vigilant for a week or so. But then they went back to their ways, leaving doors unlocked and keys in cars.

She'd missed this town. She'd been gone nearly ten years, only returning for holidays and a few weeks each summer. She'd missed her brothers. She'd missed rodeos. She'd missed graduating high school with friends. They'd all moved on in her absence. Many of them were married now. Several had moved away. They had children and homes of their own.

Why had she thought she could come home and everything would be as it had been when she left? No, she hadn't left. She'd been sent away. Banished. And nothing had stayed the same. Her brothers, the town, the people she'd known—everyone was different.

She was different.

Pushing aside those thoughts, she stood on the sidewalk and stretched, loosening her muscles and preparing mentally for a run that would shake her loose from memories. Thanks to Remington's appearance at the hospital, he was front and center in her mind.

The door to Duke's opened. She was surprised to see her brother.

"Just getting off work?" he asked as he walked down the steps. Duke was a big guy, closer to seven feet than six. He was all muscle. And all heart. She'd been angry with him for a long time because she'd wanted him to take her side and keep her here, at home.

"Yeah. You?"

He didn't answer right away. She stopped stretching and glanced his way, saw that he was watching her with eyes narrowed.

"Bad day?" he asked.

She shook her head and finished stretching before giving him her full attention. "No worse than any other. I just felt like I needed to run."

"No one understands that better than me." Because Duke had struggled when he first came home from Afghanistan. "Remington came in for dinner. With Gus. I guess he's moving back to town."

So many questions without actually asking.

"Why are you open so late?" she asked, ignoring the obvious. She didn't want to discuss Remington.

"Late dinner crowd. There was a softball game and everyone came in after."

Summer, rodeos and softball. The three went together in Martin's Crossing. Samantha took a deep breath of summer air perfumed with flowers, sultry humidity and farmland.

"Go home to your family, Duke. I'm good."

He watched her for another long minute. "You're sure?"

"I'm sure. I know Remington is back. I saw him at the hospital today. I survived. I'm running because I don't feel like going home to an empty house."

"Come down and visit us, then," he offered.

She laughed. "Because Oregon and Lilly want company this late at night? I don't think so. Go home."

"I'll go but you text me or call when you get home. If you don't, I'll have to come looking for you."

She loved his protectiveness. "I'll text you."

He gave her a tight hug, then headed around the back of the building where he'd parked his truck. Samantha watched him go, then took off running down the sidewalk. She headed down Main Street to the intersection. Ahead of her the Community Church was dark and quiet, bathed only in the orange glow of streetlights. The park was equally dark. She kept running, breathing in deep and letting go of the tenseness that had built up during the long day.

She loved working with children. She wouldn't change jobs for anything. But watching those children in pain was tough. She'd tried but couldn't leave her work behind at the end of the day. Parker, Danny and the others, they were in her heart. She knew that the longer she remained in this job, the more she'd have to cry about.

She ran several miles, keeping to the few side streets that made up Martin's Crossing. As she turned back up Main Street, she saw a truck had parked next to hers. She slowed her steps, going from a run to a jog and then a walk.

The driver of the truck got out. Even on the dimly lit street, she knew him. She knew the way he stood. She knew the way he pushed that white cowboy hat back. He shouldn't be so familiar to her. But he was.

"What are you doing here?" she asked as she leaned over to touch her toes. When she straightened, he was leaning against the side of his truck, watching her.

"I would have gone running with you if you'd called," he said.

She looked him over. Jeans, cowboy hat, boots. Her heart did a little flip she had to ignore. "Really?"

"I would have changed."

She lifted one shoulder. "I like to run alone."

That was what had changed about her in the years since she'd been sent away. She'd gotten used to being alone. She'd gone from the girl at the center of the crowd to a woman who knew how to be independent.

"Of course." He sat on the tailgate of his truck. "I was driving through town and I saw you running. I didn't like the idea of leaving you here alone."

"I'm a big girl. No one needs to protect me or rescue me."

The words slipped out and she wished she'd kept quiet. Not that he would understand what she meant. He wouldn't guess that she'd waited for him to rescue her from her aunt Mavis, believing he'd show up and take her away. She'd thought they would be a family.

But he hadn't rescued her. There hadn't been a letter or a phone call. Not once in all of those years had she ever heard from him.

That summer she'd learned an important lesson about love. Remington had said he loved her. Her brothers had said they loved her and that's why they'd sent her away. Her mom should have loved her. She'd left when Samantha was little more than a baby.

Now it was all just water under the bridge.

"Sam?" The quiet, husky voice broke into her thoughts.

So much for letting go of the tension. She faced the man who had broken her fifteen-year-old heart.

"Remington, I don't want to do this. I don't want to talk about what happened. I don't want to figure out the past. I'm building a future for myself. I have a job I love. I have a home, my family and a life I'm reclaiming. Don't make this about what happened before, because I don't want to go back."

He held up his hands in surrender. "I know. I promise, I'm here to talk about the future. Sit down, please."

She paced a few steps away from him, then faced him again. "I don't want to sit."

"Stubborn as always." He grinned as he said it, his teeth flashing white in his suntanned face.

"Not stubborn. I just don't want to sit down."

"I'm sorry they sent you away," he spoke quietly. In the distance coyotes howled and a train whistle echoed in the night. His words were soft, shifting things inside her that she didn't want shifted. Like the walls she'd built up around her.

"Me, too." She rubbed her hands down her suddenly chilled arms. "I wasn't prepared to see you today."

She opened her mouth to tell him more, but she couldn't. Not yet. Not tonight. There was more to tell him. She'd tried to write him a letter. More than once she'd sat down with pen and paper and tried to tell him everything that had happened. At sixteen she hadn't found the right words. At seventeen she'd wanted to put it all behind her. As she got older, she'd convinced herself he didn't need to know.

Maybe Aunt Mavis had been right. They'd been kids ten years ago. What did two kids know about love and forever? It had been a learning experience. A mistake.

"We should talk."

She gave up and sat down next to him on the metal tailgate. "Rem, I'm just not ready for this. I know I've had plenty of time to come to terms with what happened, but I'm just not ready to talk it all out with you yet."

"I'm sorry. I always thought eventually we'd run into each other here in Martin's Crossing. It took longer than I expected."

She pulled one leg up, resting her chin on her knee. "I always looked for you. When I came home for breaks, I'd drive by Gus's, thinking you might be there."

"I looked for you, too. Now it seems as if we're both back in town for good."

She looked up, surprised. "For good? You're staying here?"

In the light of the street lamp she saw the twinkle in his eyes. "Gus needs my help on the ranch. And now Parker and his grandmother are moving in."

"So you're moving here?"

"I'm going to pastor the Countryside Church and run the ranch."

"I see." But she didn't. It was all well and good to see him at the hospital with a horse named John Wayne. She'd never expected him back in Martin's Crossing. Back in her life.

Remington let the silence linger around them. He guessed they both had their memories of that summer. From his point of view, he'd been a kid who'd fallen hard for a pretty girl. They'd been young and they'd gone too far too fast. He'd faced the wrath of Jake and Duke Martin. They'd run him off the ranch and out of her life, letting him know he wasn't welcome on Martin land, or near their sister. Gus had sent him back home to his folks, and their ranch near Austin, where his mom told him to learn from his mistakes.

Samantha Martin. Sitting next to her now on the tailgate, he felt the past coming at him like a steam train. Her arm brushed against his, her soft scent tangled with the breeze and attempted to drive him crazy.

Common sense told him not to go back down that road. He remembered all too well how it had felt to be sent packing. As an adult he doubted her brothers would be his problem. No, if he had any intentions of pursuing her, she'd be the one sending him away.

"*Pastor* Jenkins?" she said it with a teasing glint in her eyes.

"Yeah, surprise." He shifted to look at her. "There I was in college studying agriculture and taking a class on the Bible that was meant to be an easy A. Instead I found something I'd been missing. I didn't mean for it to be a career."

"I haven't gone to church in ages." Her voice was soft, a little bit lost and all kinds of hurt.

He didn't know what to say to that. He knew she probably had her reasons for not going to church and he didn't want to push for answers. He'd learned a hard lesson a few years ago about dating, and found out that if two people lived on opposite sides of the faith fence, it was difficult to make a relationship work.

They sat there a few more minutes. "Parker is your cousin?" she asked.

"Yeah. I guess you know his parents died in a car accident?"

"Yes, I knew. I'm sorry."

"Me, too. It's going to be tough on him. And on his grandmother, my aunt Lee."

"But they have you. And Gus."

Yes, they had him. He hadn't really planned this, coming back to Martin's Crossing. Life was funny that way. It never really went according to plan. At least not his. At seventeen he'd planned on marrying the woman sitting next to him.

"How is your granddad?" she asked, dragging him back to the present.

"Slowing down, but he's good. He's recovered from his stroke and thinks he can still outwork me. My mom worries about him."

"It's good that you can be here to help him. To help them." Meaning his aunt and Parker.

Her fingers momentarily closed over his, then let go.

He hadn't expected that. He also didn't expect her to hop down from the tailgate and take off. He watched her go. She didn't head for her truck. Instead she headed down the street, walking slow and easy.

"What are you doing?" he called out to her.

She glanced back, a finger pressed to her lips. Okay, silence, he got that. He followed her. Suddenly she was on all fours, peeking under the truck parked in front of Lefty Mueller's woodworking shop.

"Come here, sweetheart. Come on," she said in a sweet tone that would have had him crawling through hot coals to get to her.

"What…"

She shot him a look and shook her head. Right. No talking.

He saw what had drawn her attention. A pregnant hound dog, skin and bones but about to whelp any day. The dog whimpered, then crawled out from under the truck. Sam sat back on her heels and the dog nuzzled into her lap, all big brown eyes and long ears.

"What are you going to do with her?"

Sam held the hound's soulful face in her hands. "Take her home."

"Duke and Jake will love that."

"Duke and Jake don't have a say in the matter. I'm not going to ask their opinion on every decision I make."

"Or any decision," he muttered, heading for his truck.

"You're leaving?" she called out, sounding like she honestly didn't want him to go.

He shook his head. "No, I'm getting you a lead rope for your new pet."

When he returned with the rope she was standing, the underfed and overly pregnant dog standing next to her. He shook his head and handed her the rope.

"What?" She made a loop and put the rope around the dog's neck.

"I'm just thinking that you're asking for trouble."

"She's beautiful." Sam brushed a hand down the dog's head. "Maybe part bloodhound?"

Beautiful. He had to agree. Standing there in shorts, a T-shirt and with her hair pulled back, Sam was beautiful. He let himself get tangled up in everything he'd felt years ago. But those memories would get him nowhere. He pushed his hat back and refocused his attention on the dog.

"From the looks of that face and those ears, I'd say yes," he agreed, reaching to let the dog sniff his hand.

"Who would dump a pretty girl like her?"

"Someone tired of puppies would be my guess."

"Then they should have gotten her fixed."

"I agree. I'm just giving you my opinion on why she's been left on the side of the road."

"Yes, because she's going to have puppies." Her expression changed from angry to something close to sad, then she walked away, the dog next to her. He watched them go, wondering what that look meant and fearing deep down that he didn't know the whole story.

"Maybe she just got lost?"

Back at her truck, Sam opened the door and coaxed the dog inside. "That's a possibility."

"We can ask around. Someone might be missing her."

"Yes, I'll do that. I'll put a poster up at Duke's and at the grocery store."

Inside the truck the dog had settled on the seat, happy to be inside. Sam fidgeted, her bottom lip caught between her teeth.

Ten years. They had become different people. They no longer knew each other. If he was honest, he'd admit they'd probably never known each other. They'd been kids. They'd both liked horses, rodeos and sitting down by the creek on a summer day.

It hadn't been a relationship, his mom had informed him. It had been a summer romance.

The warm night air reminded him that it was summer once again. With that thought in mind, he had to head home, because now was the wrong time for him to get distracted.

"Thanks for..." she started at the same time he said, "I should go."

"Goodbye, Rem. I'm glad we talked."

"Yeah, me, too."

She walked away from him and he watched her go. After she'd driven away, he sat on the tailgate of his truck for a while, thinking about that summer, about being seventeen and really believing he knew everything about life.

He hadn't had a clue. He still didn't have a clue. But he knew that Samantha Martin was in his past. That's where she belonged. And that's where a wise man would leave her.

He was smart, but he'd never been too wise.

Chapter Three

Samantha woke up early the next morning. She loved waking up on the ranch, to the quiet broken only by country sounds. Dogs, a cow in the distance, a tractor working in a nearby field. Carrying her cup of coffee, she walked out to the barn.

After she'd gotten home last night, she'd put the pregnant dog in a stall with a bowl of leftover stew and a bucket of water. As she headed across the yard she could hear the animal whining.

"What's going on, pretty girl?" She leaned across the top of the stall and peeked in. "Oh, I see."

The dog yelped and turned to clean her new puppies. There were four already, still damp and squirmy. The mamma dog hovered over them, nervous about having company.

"Hey, what's up?" A loud, chipper voice burst into the moment.

Lilly. Sam turned to greet her niece, Duke's daughter. The surprise, as Sam liked to call her. Duke hadn't known about his daughter until just last year. Sam loved the bubbly, energetic twelve-year-old. She secretly hoped the girl would keep Duke on his toes.

Sam held up a finger, and then pointed to the stall. "Shhh."

Lilly silently tiptoed forward, her eyes going big when she looked inside and saw the dog. And now, five puppies.

"We should give her some privacy," Sam said. "Let's have breakfast."

As soon as the two of them walked out of the barn, Lilly's carefully contained energy uncorked. "Where did you get her? What's her name? And did you know my mom is going to adopt a baby?"

Sam blinked a few times. Okay, this was news. And probably not the way Duke or Oregon wanted it announced.

"I'm not sure what to say, Lilly." Sam cleared her throat. "You know, your parents might not want everyone to know."

"Mom said I could tell you."

"Oh, well that's good. I didn't know and I'm excited for them."

"It's through the state. He's only six weeks old and he's living in a foster home in Houston. We're going to see him next week."

"That's amazing. I can't wait to meet him."

"Me, too." Lilly glanced back at the barn. "So, where did you get the dog?"

"I found her in town."

"Oh, that's the dog that my dad was talking about. The stray that he's going to have to do something about."

"He said that?"

"You know how guys are," Lilly said, rolling her eyes.

"Yes, I do know how guys are. And he isn't going to do anything about this dog because she's mine now."

Lilly just shrugged. "So, I'm out of school and bored."

Sam laughed. "I'm sure you are. What are you going to do with your summer?"

Lilly shrugged and Sam got the feeling there was more she wanted to say. They kept walking, though, back to the house. Sam hadn't been here when Oregon and Lilly showed up a few years ago. When Duke learned that the precocious girl across the street was his daughter. But she was here now. And she loved being an aunt.

"So?" she prodded her niece. "Give it up. I know you have more to say. Or something to ask."

"Okay. Dad said you were the best barrel racer in the county. I'm not the best. But I want to be. I'll be thirteen soon and I don't want to have to compete with the little girls."

"Gotcha. So we have some work to do?"

Lilly nodded. "Please. I mean, Dad tries to help me, but he's a guy. He can rope. He can train a horse."

"But he isn't a barrel racer."

"Right." Lilly stepped through the door Sam opened.

"That works for me, because my new gelding needs some practice." Sam followed her niece inside. The kitchen felt cool after being outside. It was not quite nine o'clock and already hot and humid. "Want breakfast?"

In answer Lilly headed for the cabinet, helping herself to cereal bars. She and Oregon had lived in this house for a time. The girl knew her way around more than just the house. She knew how to be a part of the Martin family. Sam envied that. Sometimes she felt like the outsider, as if she was the one who didn't know how to be a Martin.

"Are you going to eat?" Lilly poured herself a glass of milk and dunked the cereal bar.

"Not yet. I need at least another cup or two of coffee." She poured herself a cup and leaned against the counter next to Lilly. "About this horse business. I have to work this evening, but I can help you this morning. We might even trailer the horses over to the rodeo grounds. I always found it helpful to get away from the ranch arena."

"Really? You'd do that?"

"Of course. You're my niece and we have a tradition to continue in this family."

Lilly popped the last bite in her mouth, and then drained the glass of milk. She wiped her mouth with a paper towel and put the glass in the sink. "So, you're going to barrel race this summer?"

"We'll see how things go."

"Do you think we should go check on your dog?" Lilly glanced toward the barn. "Have you named her?"

"Not yet. I don't want to name her if she belongs to someone and she's just lost. I'll put up some posters and see if anyone claims her. As a matter of fact, let me get my phone so I can take a picture."

They were on their way to the barn when Jake pulled up. Sam waved at her brother, but she and Lilly kept walking. She knew he'd follow. She also knew he'd have something to say about the stray dog.

As she and Lilly leaned over, watching the mama dog and her litter of six, Jake stepped into the barn.

"What do we have here?" He sidled next to her and groaned when he saw the dog and puppies. "A stray?"

"No, she's not a stray. She either belongs to someone or she's mine. She's not a stray."

He cleared his throat. "She's a mutt."

"Jake, I don't have to ask your permission to get a dog." She wouldn't argue with him. Not in front of Lilly.

She wanted to tell her brother that what she did was no longer his business. He didn't get to make decisions about her life, her career, who she dated. Not that she had dated since she'd come home. But she definitely got no say in what animals she brought home. He'd made decisions for her when she was younger and hadn't asked her opinion. No more.

"You're right. You don't," he said just as quietly. "I just wanted to let you know, Breezy isn't feeling too great. The baby is fussy. I think they're both going to need a trip to the doctor."

"I can watch the twins for you," she was quick to offer.

"Marty has them, but if she needs a break, can she call you?"

"You know she can."

Lilly glanced at Jake, then at Sam. "Do I need to leave so you two can argue?"

Sam laughed a little and Jake looked uncomfortable.

"You stay put, kiddo. Aunt Sam and I will step outside."

Brothers. She gave Lilly a quick wink and the girl shook her head, as if she got it. Because even though she didn't have brothers, she had Duke for a dad.

"Back in a minute, Lilly," she assured her niece.

"If you need me to rescue you, the code word is *help*."

Sam laughed. "I'll remember that."

Jake was waiting for her outside. They walked to the fence, neither saying a word. Sam leaned her arms across the top rail and watched her new gelding, a pretty palomino, as he trotted across the field, his buttery gold coat soaking up the sunshine. Standing next to Jake, she felt small. And young. She exhaled her frustration, but he didn't react.

"Nice horse," Jake commented.

"What do you want, Jake?"

"I ran across Remington. He was at the feed store."

"Yeah, he lives here now."

He cleared his throat. "So you know he's in town?"

"Yes, I know." She could have said more, but she didn't want to make this easy for him. She didn't want to let him off the hook. Her brothers had hurt her. They'd meant to protect her, to make things right. But they'd hurt her along the way.

It still ached. Not the way it had before, but from time to time it would sneak up on her. She closed her eyes tight for a moment, long enough to fight back the tears.

Jake touched her back. "I'm sorry, Sam. I don't know what else to say. We were young. We were doing the best we could. And we didn't know how to raise a younger sister."

"I know. So why did you feel the need to tell me you saw Remington?"

"I didn't want you to be surprised."

"Oh, I was surprised. He showed up at the hospital with a crew of cowboys who minister to kids."

"Ah."

He said it as though he understood. She doubted he did. He hadn't lived with Aunt Mavis. He hadn't lived through the Bible lessons, the lectures and the condemnation.

She'd always thought her aunt well-meaning. She'd given the older woman the benefit of the doubt. That didn't ease the pain.

"I should go. Lilly is in there with the dog and she wants me to help her with her horse."

Before she could step away, Jake stopped her, his hand on her arm. "Sam, we're all glad you're home. We want you here. But we want more than that. We want you in our lives."

She nodded but her throat was tight and tears burned her eyes. "I know. I don't go to work until three. I can watch the twins if you need me to."

The twins. Rosie and Violet. They were the daughters of Jake's twin, Elizabeth. She and her husband had died in a plane crash, devastating the family all over again. They'd had too much devastation in their past. A mother who had walked away. A father who drank himself to death. Then Elizabeth's death.

But they were making up for those hard times. Jake had found Breezy, the sister of Elizabeth's husband, Lawton. Duke and Oregon had found each other. Brody had Grace.

They all had someone. Except her.

Sam shook off the melancholy. She had her family. And that was good.

She was saved from darker thoughts when Lilly ran out of the barn, a big grin on her face. "Nine. There are nine puppies!"

"I should go home and leave the two of you to your labor and delivery." Jake leaned to kiss Sam's cheek. "Let me know if you need anything."

"Will do." She glanced away, hoping he didn't see the truth. She needed him. She needed all of her brothers.

"Sam, I hope you'll forgive us."

She stopped, unsure of how to process that request. She was forced to look at Jake, to see the tenderness in his expression. She nodded, brushing hair back from her face as the wind kicked up. She started to tell him there was nothing to forgive, but it didn't seem honest. She'd been angry with them. She loved her brothers, but they'd hurt her.

"I'm working on it," she said. It was a candid answer and he seemed to accept it.

"Good. That's all we ask."

When he left, she headed for the barn and Lilly. What she needed was an hour or two on horseback to clear her mind.

Remington had spent his morning with a family that had lost a father during the night. It hadn't been easy, watching them say goodbye to a man they'd expected to be in their lives for years to come. As much as he loved ministry, he was still adjusting to this part of the job. Standing in front of a crowd on a Sunday morning was easy compared to sitting one-on-one with a wife, telling her God would help her through the coming days, weeks and months.

He slowed as he drove past the Martin's Crossing Saddle Club. He recognized the truck with the horse trailer hooked to it, and the woman sitting on the showy palomino. Good old common sense told him to keep driving. He sure didn't need distractions in the form of Samantha Martin. He didn't need to get caught up in the past when he had the present to concern himself with.

Good advice, but he couldn't quite make himself listen. The past six hours had drained him. Seeing Sam, even from a distance, shifted things.

He hit his brakes at the first road and headed back in the direction of the rodeo grounds. He spent the next few minutes telling himself all the reasons he should let it go. Let *her* go.

He still took the road that led to the saddle club. Because the girl he'd known ten years ago was buried inside the composed shell of the woman he'd met yesterday. The wild teenager who'd grabbed hold of every adventure, who could race him across the field and never stop laughing as she beat him, she was in there somewhere.

Didn't anyone else realize that the real Samantha Martin was missing, replaced by this stranger?

He parked, got out of his truck and headed toward the arena. Sam stood next to her niece Lilly as the younger girl settled into the saddle of her horse. She glanced his way, shook her head and went back to the conversation she'd been having. Lilly held the reins in one hand and patted the neck of the chestnut gelding with the other. She smiled big, as if being there with Sam was better than Christmas.

The two talked for a minute, then Sam said something. Lilly moved her left foot from the stirrup and Sam swung onto the back of the gelding and sat behind Lilly. Remington watched as the two walked around the barrels. At each one Sam would lean into the turn, moving Lilly with her.

Two times they went around the barrels like that, and then Sam dismounted, landing lightly next to the horse. She patted Lilly's leg and faced him.

"We weren't expecting an audience," Sam said as she walked past him to her gelding that she'd tied to the gate.

"I drove by and then thought…" He left the words hanging. He didn't know what he'd thought. But here he was. He could fight it, but the attraction was still there. It felt like they were tethered together, like her blue eyes were the only eyes he should ever look into. He could get lost in those eyes, in the emotions that flickered through them.

"You thought what?" She leaned against the fence, still inside the arena.

"I thought I'd see what you were doing and how your dog is. I guess she had her puppies?" He headed for neutral territory, which was a lot easier than admitting he'd been a little wrung out from the time spent with a grieving family and he'd been drawn to see her.

"How'd you know she had her puppies?"

"I saw Brody earlier. He was heading to Dallas."

She watched Lilly, pretending for the moment that she hadn't heard him. He'd seen the slight shift in expression, the indrawn breath.

"It's Brody's business if he wants to visit Sylvia," she finally answered. "But that isn't why you're here, is it?"

"No, it isn't."

She continued to watch her niece. The breeze picked up and Sam pushed her hair back, holding it in place as it tried to sweep across her cheek. Lilly rode up to them, pulling her horse in as she got close.

"Take him again. And this time with some speed. You have to trust your horse, Lilly."

"Trust my horse. Got it." Lilly grinned big at Sam and then at him.

"Go," Sam warned her niece. The girl turned the horse and rode away. "So, why are you here?"

"I'm not really sure," he said, watching her niece take the barrels. "No, that isn't entirely true. I had a rough night with a family from Jamesville. I saw you down here and thought I'd stop and say hello."

Her hand touched his arm. "The car accident?"

"Yeah." He didn't know what else to say.

"I'm sorry. It doesn't get any easier, does it?" Being a nurse, she would know how it felt to lose someone, to feel helpless and as if words were empty and meaningless in the face of someone's grief.

"No, it doesn't," he agreed.

She looked away, focusing on her niece, calling out a few pointers.

"She's doing better this time," he said as he watched Lilly take the barrels again. He saw her confidence kick in as the chestnut made good time and she brought the gelding home faster than the previous run.

Sam noticed and she nodded. She cheered as her niece pulled the horse up. "Now that was a ride, Lilly. You're going to be tough to beat."

"Thanks, Aunt Sam." Lilly leaned down, hugging the neck of her horse.

"Walk him around the arena, let him cool off, and then we'll head back to the ranch."

Sam faced him then. "By the way, I have nine puppies. Since you were there, I hold you responsible for finding homes for at least four of them."

He held up his hands and shook his head. "I had nothing to do with that mess."

She grinned and it undid the tension he'd been feeling since the start of the conversation. When she looked at him like that, it felt like the sun coming out after a month of rain.

"You were there, Rem. You share the blame and the responsibility." And then the sun went behind the clouds. Her eyes shadowed and it seemed as if with one sentence she took on the weight of the world.

"Sam?"

"I have to go. Lilly needs me."

As she walked away, heading for the gate opposite where they stood, he hurried around the arena to catch up with her. He couldn't let her get away, not now, when it seemed they had things to say to one another.

But Lilly was there, unsaddling the horse she'd tied to the trailer, and Sam was smiling, pretending he hadn't unleashed something deep inside her. He watched as the two of them discussed Lilly's horse and how well she'd done. Lilly asked if Sam was going to ride her horse again. The palomino was still saddled and tied to the gate.

"No, I think he's had enough for the day. So have I. We should head back to the ranch and have some lunch before I have to go in to work."

That was his cue to stop standing around like a self-conscious kid trying to work up the nerve to ask out the most popular girl in school.

"I need to get back to Gus. He's trying to fix a tractor he should have replaced twenty years ago." He backed away from them. Sam lifted the saddle off her horse and settled it on the saddle rack.

She faced him again, her blue eyes the color of a perfect spring day. Yeah, she still made him wax poetic. He had written her a few poems. Really bad ones, if memory served. He doubted she'd kept his poetry that compared her hair to corn silk and her lips to cotton candy.

"What are you smiling about?"

He should have said nothing. Instead he pulled off his hat and laughed. "Your hair is the color of corn silk and your eyes the color of robin's eggs."

"I can't believe you remember that. You were the worst poet in the world. I take that back. You were no poet, Mr. Jenkins. There is nothing about my lips that resembles cotton candy."

But at least she was laughing. He guessed he'd have to add a line about her laughter being like the chorus of songbirds, or something equally corny.

"No, I wasn't a poet. But I'm sure that even my lack of poetic ability didn't detract from my charming personality."

"Yes, you were charming."

"So the two of you dated?" Lilly stopped brushing her horse and looked at them. "Seriously?"

"Seriously," Sam answered. "It was a long time ago."

"I should go," he said.

She nodded in agreement. "Give Gus my love. If he needs anything, tell him to call."

"I'll tell him."

She walked away, a cowgirl in a pale pink T-shirt and faded jeans that he'd never quite forgotten.

Chapter Four

On the last day of Sam's four-day workweek, Dr. Jackson called her into his office. She stepped into the tiny room, files and papers stacked everywhere. Sitting behind his desk, he motioned for her to take a seat. She moved a few files from the chair and sat down to wait. He didn't speak for a moment. His gray head was bent as he read over a manual of some type and he was clearly puzzled. After a few minutes, he shook his head.

"Have you ever put an entertainment center together?" he asked without looking up.

She laughed, because she'd thought he might be studying a new medical procedure or a research paper. He glanced up, his glasses perched on the end of his nose.

"That's funny?" he asked.

"Yes, I thought this was about a patient. A treatment. Not an entertainment system. In answer to your question, yes, I have."

"Of course you have. That's something I like about you, Samantha, you're independent." He slid the paper across his cluttered desk. "Why does this seem wrong?"

She gave it a look and then turned it over and held it

up to the light. "Because it's backwards. Right to left, not left to right."

"Gotcha." He took the paper back and held it up to the light. "Well, I'll be dipped in tartar sauce."

That was a new one. He did like to make up his own sayings and the nurses all repeated them. She couldn't wait to share "dipped in tartar sauce." She waited for him to say more.

He looked up again and removed his glasses. "You live in Martin's Crossing, correct?"

"Yes, sir."

"That's what I thought." He reached for a file and pushed the glasses back on his face. "Parker."

Her mood lifted, because Parker had that effect on people. He'd gone through so much but still had a way of making others a little bit happier.

"What about Parker?"

"As you know, he's going home," he handed her the file. "Today."

"I knew he'd be released soon but didn't realize it would be today. That's wonderful." But also frightening. She always worried when a patient went home.

"Yes, it is. But we're not ready to turn him loose. Not completely. Which is why we've come up with a new service we'd like to do on a trial basis."

"New service?" She really had no idea how this pertained to her.

"Yes, we'd like to do a continued care program for our patients."

Home visits. Good idea. But then she realized why she'd been called in to the office. She lived in Martin's Crossing, which meant he wanted her to look in on Parker. She looked at the file, then met the serious gaze of the man sitting across the desk from her. He must have seen on her face that she planned to object because he held up a hand to stop her.

"We need someone to check on him once a week. Nothing too time-consuming. A short visit to make sure he's still progressing and coping with the home environment. Also to make sure the caregivers—the family—are coping. I think if we do this, we can catch infections and other issues before they become problems that could jeopardize the health and continued recovery of our patients."

Brilliant idea really, but the thought of stopping by the Jenkins farm every week wasn't really one she wanted to embrace.

"I think it's a great idea. But someone else should do it," she started.

"You live in Martin's Crossing. Parker thinks you're the best nurse ever. And I have confidence in you because you have experience in several areas."

"Yes, but…" she started. Then stopped. What could she say to that?

"Is something wrong?"

She shook her head. "No, nothing is wrong."

"Great, then we'll get all of the appropriate paperwork taken care of. We'll need you to keep track of your time and mileage."

"Of course."

He stood and rounded the desk. "Let's go talk to his family."

She could tell by his tone and expression that in his mind it was all settled. Because he didn't know how much she wanted to avoid Remington Jenkins. He didn't know how much it hurt to look at Remington and remember.

She chased away that thought because this was about

a child. And children came first. Parker came first. He came before her fears, her doubts and her resentment.

When they got to Parker's room, they found it filled with staff and family. Parker sat in his wheelchair with a big grin on his face and a new cowboy hat on his head. His grin grew even wider, if possible, when he saw that he had more guests for his going-home party. Every child who left the hospital got a party as a farewell and a celebration.

"Nurse Sam, look—I got a hat! And new boots. And I'll have a new room at Uncle Gus's."

"I heard, Parker. I'm so excited for you." She moved through the crowd, smiling at Gus and at Parker's grandmother. Then her heart stuttered a bit when she made eye contact with Remington. He stood to the side, casually leaning against the wall, his arms crossed over his chest.

At that moment, she considered telling Dr. Jackson why it was impossible for her to take this job. But what would she say? That she'd been fifteen and crazy in love with a cowboy that her brothers didn't approve of? That she'd been sent away from home and the cowboy had been sent packing, back to his parents in Austin?

It sounded like a romance novel. Young love. A broken heart. No big deal. To anyone but her. So she shoved it all aside because she wasn't going to let it determine her future or the future of a boy who needed every opportunity to succeed.

She stepped in front of Parker, lowering herself to his level, accepting his big hug. Face-to-face with the child, her objections gave up their last stand of resistance. For Parker, for the other children, she would do whatever was necessary.

"You take care of yourself. And no stunts," she warned.

"Ah, Nurse Sam, you know I'm not going to be good."

She laughed at his honesty. "At least be safe."

"I can do that."

"And I'm going to stop by and check on you in a few days so you don't miss us too much."

"That's great," he said. "I can show you the ranch. And someday I can see the ranch where you live. And I'll go to school there in a few months."

"Super. I have a niece who goes to school in Martin's Crossing. She's a few years older than you, but I'm sure she'll show you around."

"Does she ride horses? Remington said everyone in Martin's Crossing rides. I'm sure I could learn to ride."

"Let's take one thing at a time, Parker." His grandmother moved to his side, her look a little unsure, Sam thought. But of course she was. She was going to raise this little guy. It had been only a few months since the accident that took his parents. Just a few months of healing and learning a new way of living.

"Oh, Granny, I know that. It'll be okay."

Big words from a little boy. He reached for his grandmother's hand and held it tight.

"We should go," his grandmother said. She moved behind his wheelchair. "We have a lot to do when we get home."

"Like have burgers on the grill," Parker said. "Rem and Uncle Gus are cooking tonight. You should come over, Nurse Sam."

"Oh, no, that's okay. You'll have a lot to do, getting settled. I'll be by soon enough."

"You're more than welcome to join us tonight," his grandmother offered. "I know Parker thinks the world of you. We're all so glad you're going to continue to be involved in his care."

"I'm glad, too." Out of the corner of her eye she

saw Remington push away from the wall. He moved around the room, grabbing the suitcase and a box that held Parker's prized possessions. "Okay, Parker, time for you to say your final goodbyes and head home."

Parker looked around the room that had been his for several very long weeks, his expression suddenly showing the case of nerves he'd been hiding. He bit down on his bottom lip and nodded. "I'm ready."

"You'll do great, tiger." Dr. Jackson placed a hand on his shoulder. "We'll walk you out."

As they exited the room, the real party started. The children and nurses were lined up and down the hall with balloons, noisemakers and hats. Parker laughed, waving at his friends. He stopped a few times for extra hugs from staff who had taken care of him through the long months of recovery and rehab.

Sam walked along behind the group. On her way out the door Dr. Jackson had asked her to escort the family to their car and get them all settled. If she didn't know better, she'd think the man was plotting against her.

Remington walked alongside her.

"I had no idea going home would be like this," he said.

"We try to make it a special occasion."

"Thank you for taking us on. I know it means the world to Parker, to know that you'll still be in his life."

She kept walking, following the slow procession of Parker, his grandmother, Gus and Dr. Jackson as they made their way down the hall toward the double doors, the lobby and then to the front exit. She took the bag that Remington carried, lightening his load.

"The invitation stands, if you'd like to join us for burgers on the grill," he continued.

She glanced up, into gray eyes that she knew so well. "I don't think so."

"We're going to have to get used to being around one another. You might find—" he grinned as he said it "—that you *want* to spend more time with me."

"I doubt that." She bit back the smile he probably expected. "I'm not interested in going back and revisiting my fifteen-year-old self. She was a mess."

"I remember liking her a lot but I understand not wanting to revisit those days. But it won't hurt for us to be friends right now."

"No, it won't hurt." But she worried it might.

There was so much more between them. More than he realized.

Remington glanced at the woman walking next to him. He'd give anything to know why her expression seemed so troubled and why something as simple as friendship set her on edge. Yes, they shared a past. It wasn't as if they were enemy states trying to find a way to sign a peace treaty.

He knew one thing: pushing wasn't going to get him anywhere with Samantha Martin. He guessed she'd been pushed enough. Pushed away from him, from her home, away from everything safe and familiar.

He'd just gone home to Austin and his family.

Gus said she'd never been the same. She'd come home from time to time. Every now and then she'd ridden in a local rodeo or eaten dinner at her brother's diner, but she hadn't been the girl he'd known in Martin's Crossing.

Gus said she was angry and bitter.

Remington saw it as pain. Deep down pain. He saw a woman who was willing to help animals and children but wasn't as willing to let people into her life.

He watched as she helped Aunt Lee put Parker in the

car, something Lee had been learning to do in rehab. For
the past month his aunt had worked with the staff because there would be things she'd have to do for Parker.
He and Gus would help her. They'd given their word
they wouldn't let her do this alone. But they all knew
that most of it would fall on Parker's grandmother.

Which is why it made sense for him to give up his
job in Austin and settle here on his granddad's ranch,
the Rocking J. To help Gus, Aunt Lee and Parker.

After Parker was settled in the backseat, Sam leaned
to kiss his cheek, then she took a step back, letting his
grandmother say something to him. Dr. Jackson moved
in to share a few words. And then they called Remington forward.

"Will you pray?" Dr. Jackson asked. "I'd like to send
you all home with the best support system available."

Rem agreed. They could all use a guiding hand in
this situation. "Of course I'll pray."

His gaze strayed in Samantha's direction. She looked
away. But he saw the flicker of doubt, the anger. He
hadn't expected that.

He bowed his head and prayed. For strength, for healing, for peace. He prayed for a special blessing on the
staff that gave such great care to these children.

After he ended the prayer, he glanced her way again.
Sam's blue eyes were on him, full of questions. He had
answers, but he doubted she really wanted to hear them.
Not yet anyway.

He met her clear blue gaze. She raised her chin a
notch and walked away, back to the hospital. He told
himself not to take it too personally, but he did. He'd
never expected this reaction to his decision to go into
ministry. He'd dated a woman who didn't like that she
sometimes had to share him with others. He'd dated an-

other woman who had finally admitted she just couldn't be the wife of a pastor.

"Time to go," he said to no one in particular.

"Time to go," Parker echoed as Remington got behind the wheel.

Remington glanced in the rearview mirror and made eye contact with the little boy. He saw a flash of nervousness before Parker smiled, pretending everything was okay. Going home was a big deal. After months in the hospital, he was headed for a new life, new obstacles. Parker would make it, but no one could blame him for being lost and more than a little apprehensive.

It took twenty minutes to reach the Rocking J. The ranch had a long rutted dirt driveway. On each side of that driveway the ranch spilled out as far as the eye could see. It was Texas Hill Country, so the terrain was rugged and a good portion of the thousand-acre ranch was hilly with clear creeks and plenty of trees. It was about the prettiest place Remington knew.

"This is a ranch!" Parker exclaimed from the backseat. "I'm going to live on a real ranch."

"Yes, sir, you are," Gus answered. "We'll make sure you have a few cows of your own so you can start your own herd. Rem started his own herd that way. He has one here and one on his folks' place."

"I'll have my own cows?" Parker whistled. "And a horse?"

"One thing at a time, Parker." His grandmother brought him back down to earth. "Let's focus on you getting better."

"I'm better, Granny. I am. I can feel my toes sometimes and Dr. Jackson said someday I might be able to use crutches. He said not real good. But maybe a little."

Remington glanced in the rearview mirror and

caught the look on his aunt's face. She was nervous. She wanted the best for Parker. She also didn't want him to get his hopes up. His spinal injury had been in the lower portion of his back.

"Here we are." He pulled up to the two-story farmhouse with a newly built ramp.

"Wow, is this house really old?" Parker had the door open and was peering out at the land around him.

"It's not that old," Gus responded. "The original house got hit by a tornado thirty years ago and we rebuilt."

Remington left them to discuss the ranch. He retrieved Parker's wheelchair from the trunk and had it out and ready when Gus picked up the boy and settled him in the seat. Parker was still talking.

"Do you think Nurse Sam lives on a ranch like this?" he asked.

Gus shot Remington a look, a grin hidden behind his bushy mustache.

"Yeah, but bigger," Remington responded. He pushed the wheelchair toward the ramp but Parker took over, his hands on the wheels pushing hard. Remington let him go.

"You've seen where she lives?" Parker asked.

"Yes, I've seen it."

Parker stopped at the top of the porch, catching his breath. His face was a little red from the excitement and the exertion. He looked around, and then he settled that excited gaze on Remington, grinning big.

"She's the best nurse. We all think she's the prettiest."

Gus coughed as he inserted the key in the lock and pushed the front door open. Remington watched his grandfather, slightly stooped and a little bowlegged from years in the saddle. He thought about telling Gus to keep his comments—and coughs—to himself.

"You boys had too much time on your hands," Remington answered. "And now you're going to have less time and more work."

"Yeah," Parker practically shouted as he pushed himself through the front door. "And Nurse Sam will be here to check on me. Wait until I call Danny and tell him."

Remington let Aunt Lee follow the boy inside and he stayed on the front porch where there was fresh air and fewer excited statements about a certain nurse. He looked out over the ranch his father had grown up on, the ranch he'd now help his grandfather care for.

In the field beef cattle with red coats and broad backs grazed on spring grass, biting off the tender morsels. The distant crow of a rooster broke the silence. As did the sound of a car on the highway. His thoughts weren't as settled or as peaceful as his surroundings.

Samantha Martin. She wanted distance. He wanted her close. He wanted to mend fences that had been broken. If things had turned out different, he wondered if he and Sam would have dated a few years, then gotten married. Or would they have broken up after that summer? That's what his mom had predicted. She'd told him that was how most summer romances ended. It felt like something that would last forever. But usually, she'd assured him, it faded with time and distance.

He'd actually believed her until he saw Sam at the hospital.

Seeing her made it all come rushing back as if they'd never been apart. Unfortunately Sam didn't seem to feel the same way. She seemed to have put him and their relationship behind her.

He guessed he'd either have to accept that, or change her mind.

Chapter Five

Sam visited Parker the day after he'd left the hospital. It had been an easy visit, with a little boy excited by his new room, his new home and a new puppy. She'd seen the shadows in his eyes, though, and knew there were things he didn't discuss. If he pretended everything was okay, maybe they would all believe nothing had changed and they weren't grieving people who were suddenly missing in their lives.

Sam had spent too much of her life missing people. She had smiled and pretended she was whole. She'd gone to school. She'd gone to college and earned more than one degree. She'd dated a little. She'd made friends.

But something had always been missing. No, some*one* had been missing. Two someones, she realized.

Now, a week after Parker's release from the hospital, Sam had promised a visit because Parker had cows. Gus had taken him to the livestock auction and purchased five heifer calves for the boy to raise. He would have his own herd just the way Remington had promised.

She drove up the driveway of the Rocking J, maneuvering around the ruts where the dirt had been washed away by recent rains. As she got closer to the house she saw Gus, Remington and Parker at the barn.

The barn was a short walk from the house and gave her a chance to clear her head. When she got there, she was greeted by Gus, who leaned heavily on a cane. His white hair was almost as bushy as his moustache and he'd wiped a dab of grease on his jeans.

"Gus, how are you doing?" she asked, surprised to see him using the cane.

"Oh, I'm fit as a fiddle, Sammy. A little tired and sometimes a little wobbly, but I'm not going down without a fight."

"I didn't think you would." She grinned at Parker, who had pushed his chair a little closer. "And you, big shot?"

"I'm good. I even got a sunburn a few days ago." He showed her his arms.

"You'd best be using sunscreen," she warned.

He rolled his eyes at that. "Yeah, that's what my granny said. But Remington doesn't use sunscreen."

Remington picked that moment to walk out of the barn with a list that he handed Gus.

"What brings you to the Rocking J?" he asked.

"I'm here to see a new herd of cattle."

He gave her a look. "In a dress?" Remington asked.

"Sorry, I've been to town and stopped here on my way home." She turned her attention back to Parker because it was easier, dealing with him. It was easier than looking at Remington when he brought back so many memories. "So, what about those cows of yours?"

"They're in the field. Uncle Gus said by next year I'll have calves. I can build my herd that way. I'll keep the heifer calves and sell the bull calves."

"That's how I built my own herd, Parker." She squatted next to his chair. "How are you feeling today?"

"Great. Granny was surprised that I can get out of my bed on my own. She said I should wait for her."

"I'll talk to her and tell her that you're pretty good at those transfers. And you're doing your exercises?"

"Yep. Rem does those with me. Sometimes Granny."

"Good job." She lifted her gaze and caught Remington watching her, his gray eyes holding her captive for a moment. She brushed off the reaction and stood. "Let's go see those cows. How are you doing on this rough terrain? This isn't like the hospital."

"I don't mind so much. Rem usually helps me out. Yesterday we took the mule."

She stopped at that. "Mule?"

Remington nodded, indicating the ATV at the side of the barn. "Not a four-legged mule, Sam. Two rows of seats, six wheels and seat belts."

"Gotcha." Of course she should have known.

"I'm going to let the three of you go check on those heifers," Gus interrupted. "I've got to head to town. I need new tires on the livestock trailer and I have to order a few things from the feed store. And whatever Rem put on this list." He waved a bit of paper, and then shoved it in his shirt pocket.

"And have coffee at the diner?" Rem asked as he pushed Parker toward the previously mentioned mule.

Sam watched the three of them—Remington, Parker and Gus—as they discussed Gus's plans. But her gaze lingered on Remington. Standing there with him just feet away, all cowboy in his faded jeans, worn boots and T-shirt, she wasn't so sure if she should go. He was six feet of temptation and past actions had proven he was hard to resist.

He picked that moment to face her and she felt heat crawl into her face. Instead of letting it go, he winked.

Every moment she spent in Remington Jenkins's company reminded her of everything she'd lost, everything she'd given up. It reminded her that there were things they needed to talk about.

Today, though, was about Parker. It was about warm sunshine, the smell of grass and country air.

"Ready to do this?" Remington asked.

"Of course."

"You take that backseat. I'll put Parker up front. He likes to tell me how to drive." Remington lifted the little boy from his chair. "Worst backseat driver ever."

Parker laughed, and his laughter was contagious. She took a seat directly behind Remington. She preferred the back of his head to his profile. She preferred looking at the dark hair brushing his neck and not the carefree tilt of his mouth, or the just-barely crooked nose, which he'd broken bull riding at sixteen. She didn't want to see his lean, suntanned cheeks or the dark lashes that outlined his silver-gray eyes to perfection.

But then, she also didn't want the hint of aftershave that drifted back to tease her as they drove across the pasture toward the section of the Rocking J where Parker's small herd was grazing.

Along the way the mule slowed to a stop. Remington pointed in the direction of a dozen horses. Standing close to a pretty gray mare was a foal as dark as midnight. The baby noticed them watching and pranced, all legs, doing his best to show off.

"Isn't he a nice little colt?" Remington asked, easing the mule a little closer.

"Beautiful," she admitted. "How old?"

"Not quite a week."

"Really nice."

They went on and in a few minutes they topped a small rise, the ranch spreading out before them. They could see for miles in all directions. Samantha breathed in deep.

"I missed this," she admitted.

"I'm sure you have," Remington responded as he killed the engine. "I can't imagine not being in Texas."

She wondered if he'd ever, even once, thought about her after she'd been sent away. Back then, it honestly felt as if she'd lost everyone. She could feel the resentment surfacing and she wanted to push it back down. She leaned forward to talk to Parker, the little cowboy in his jeans, new boots, cowboy hat and Western shirt.

"Where's that herd of yours, Parker?" she asked.

He scanned the cattle grazing in the field ahead of them and with a shout, he pointed. Five Angus grazed among the deep red Limousin breed cattle with their Rocking J brand.

"There they are. I picked them myself. I thought it would be good to have some Angus on this ranch." He gave Remington a satisfied smirk.

"I think that's a good idea, Parker." She rested a hand on his shoulder. "You'll do great with those Angus."

"Is that what you raise?"

She nodded. "Yes, it is."

Remington restarted the mule and they headed back toward the house. Parker talked the whole way. He told her about the food Gus cooked. He told her about sleeping in his new room and the toys they'd brought him from his old house, and that's when he slipped away, into grief.

Samantha wanted to hug him, because he was a little boy and he'd lost his parents. But she could see him working hard to control tears. Remington reached over to give his shoulder a light squeeze.

"We ought to go to Duke's for dinner tonight," Remington finally said. "I think he's got steak on the menu as a special."

"Black and blue," Samantha offered.

"It's bruised?" Parker asked, glancing back at her with just the slightest glimmer of tears still hovering in his eyes.

"No, that means it has bacon and blue cheese crumbles on top."

Parker's face scrunched. "Gross. Hey, did you tell Danny that I said hi?"

"I did," she answered. "And he said hi back to you. Did the teacher come out to talk to you this week?"

Parker groaned. "Yeah. I have to do some classes with her all summer, until school starts. So I won't be way behind, she said."

They talked a little more about school. Then they were pulling up to the barn, and Remington helped Parker back into his wheelchair.

She stood back, contemplating how to remove herself from this situation that pulled her in. Because she thought the world of Parker. Remington? She wasn't really sure what she thought of him. She watched the man, who crouched next to the little boy, talking to him about his cows. He pushed his hat back and laughed at something Parker said, then he glanced her way. She nearly melted under that look.

For years he'd been something of a fantasy. A knight who would ride to her rescue. Then he'd been the man who didn't show up when she needed him. After that he'd become the empty space in her heart.

The adult Sam had written him off as a crush. A mistake. He'd been a learning experience, teaching her not to rely on other people.

But he was someone Parker could rely on. And he was the man who could still break her heart if she let down her guard for even a second.

After Remington got Parker set up in his wheelchair, he looked over at Samantha. She was standing a short distance away, her gaze on the truck she'd left parked at the house. She was thinking through her escape plan. He could see it in her eyes.

"Can you give Parker some help back to the house?" Remington asked. "He's pretty good, but every now and then he needs a little help getting over a rough patch."

She let her gaze settle on Parker. "Of course I can help."

"I can show you my room, too." Parker was already pushing himself toward the drive. "Coming?"

"Of course." She looked over to Remington. "See you later?"

He tipped his hat and nodded. "For sure."

With that she hurried after Parker, catching the handles of the chair and helping him over the rough terrain. Remington slipped through the door of the barn and into the dim silence of the building. He took a deep breath, relaxing. There were times in his life when he felt as if he knew exactly what God wanted from him. The ministry for kids had been such a time. He'd even felt good when he'd taken the church outside Martin's Crossing.

He hadn't expected Sam. Yeah, he'd thought they'd run into each other. But he'd really expected to take it in stride, as if the past was firmly in the past. He'd guessed wrong. Meeting up with Sam was like having a head-on collision.

John Wayne whinnied. The minihorse was in a small corral, waiting for a treat. Remington stopped by the feed room for a cup of apple-flavored treats. When he walked through the door at the end of the barn, John greeted him with a nudge of his head against Remington's leg. Remington pushed him back.

"Hey, stand down, John Wayne."

The horse hung his head low, but he stood still.

"That's better. If you can't be a gentleman, you don't get treats." At the word treats, the horse perked up, and he eyed Remington. "Yeah, that's what I thought."

Remington poured the treats in his hand and offered them to the horse. "You're about the most uncomplicated person in my life, old man."

John Wayne ate up the treats and gave him another look, his shaggy black forelock hanging down between his eyes, his dark ears pricked to attention. As soon as he'd finished, John walked across the corral, his tail swishing at flies.

"And the least loyal."

Remington shook his head as he walked back into the barn, latching the door behind him. He headed toward the house, noticing that Sam's truck was still there. He'd expected her to be gone.

Instead he found her on the front porch with a glass

of iced tea. He walked up to the porch that ran most of the length of the two-story house. Gus and Lee were sitting on the porch swing. Sam was sitting on a nearby rocking chair. Parker was the only one missing.

"What are you all doing?" he asked as he pulled up a rocking chair that wasn't being used.

"Waiting for you. Sam's truck won't start." Gus tossed him a set of keys. "I thought you might try."

"As if I know more about engines than you?" he asked as he grabbed the keys out of the air. "I'll give it a shot."

He headed to Sam's truck, which was parked next to his. Sam's truck was a little newer. It didn't have an extended cab but it had all the bells and whistles. He climbed behind the wheel and stuck the key in the ignition. A few clicks, then nothing. He tried again. The stereo made a crazy noise, and then the CD changer started clicking through tracks. He pulled the key from the ignition and got out.

When he got back to the porch Sam offered him a glass of iced tea, heavy on the ice. "Well?"

"I'm guessing you need a new battery."

"That truck is only a year old," she protested.

"The battery could be defective. I'm just giving you my opinion. I can get cables and jump it for you, then follow you home."

"Thank you."

That's how he ended up at her place thirty minutes later. He'd followed her home, down her long driveway and to the little cottage that had been on the Martins' property for years. He remembered this place. At one time an older couple had lived there, helping to work the ranch. Now it was Samantha's place.

There were flowers in planters bordering the sidewalks, the small front stoop and the stone patio toward the back of the house. Bird feeders hung from the front stoop roof. She parked at the back of the house. He pulled in behind her and killed the engine to his truck. It took him a minute to decide if he would just roll down the window, make his excuses and head home, or get out. He got out.

Sam was standing in the yard waiting, twisting the bracelet on her arm. It was a sign that she wanted to say something or get something over with.

Funny how memories collided, like a kid's coloring book with connect the dots, making it all a complete picture.

"I thought you might like to see those puppies," she said, heading for the barn without asking if he wanted to follow.

He followed. His twenty-seven-year-old self wasn't much better at resisting her than his seventeen-year-old self had been.

Fortunately he had a little more experience doing the right thing.

"You're quiet," she said as they walked into the barn that had probably been on the property a good hundred years. It was wood sided, weathered and smelled of hay, animals and age.

"Guess I am."

The only real talking was going on in his mind. That conversation was all about Sam, her obvious aversion to church, his ministry and the solid truth that he wouldn't give up doing what he'd been called to do. So going down this path with her again could only lead them both back to pain.

Samantha stopped at a stall and looked over. Inside was the hound dog and her nine puppies. The door was open so that the mama could go in and out. She looked up at them with soulful eyes, her long ears hanging to the ground as she covered her puppies with her big head. The puppies squirmed and whined and fought to get close to her belly.

"What are you going to do with all of those puppies?" Remington asked.

She rested her chin on her hands that held the top rail of the stall. "I guess find them homes."

"No one has claimed the momma dog?"

"No. I named her Lady."

"Of course you did," he said, smiling and leaning closer to get a better look at the puppies, and to be a little closer to Sam.

She surprised him by leaning into him, their shoulders brushing. She rested against him for a moment before clearing her throat and stepping away.

"I should let you go. They'll be waiting for you at Duke's," she said.

"They'll know to start without me. I'm not in a hurry. Why don't you tell me what was going on today? When you got to the ranch, you looked like you'd had a bad day."

She left the barn without answering. He followed, knowing she'd talk when she was good and ready. He remembered that about her. He realized there were a lot of things he remembered from that summer.

Her destination was a glider bench on the stone patio. There were flowers everywhere, climbing up the posts where bird feeders were mounted, hanging from hooks and growing in the beds that bordered the patio. The flowers were pretty, but mostly he saw a lot of plants that needed watering.

Samantha sat down and he sat next to her, setting the glider in motion. It settled into an easy rocking and she watched as butterflies hovered over a red flower. He waited. For some reason it felt as if he'd been waiting a lifetime for this moment.

Next to him she leaned back and looked up at the dusky, pink presunset sky. "It was nothing really. I just wish life could be a little easier."

"Don't we all? Sometimes it helps to talk to a friend."

"Is that what we are? Friends?"

He decided this was one of those trick questions where there wasn't any good way to respond.

"I think we're definitely friends. Or we could be."

She laughed just a little. "Good answer, Pastor Jenkins."

"Ah, *Pastor* Jenkins. And that bothers you?" He waited, wanting her to say that it didn't bother her.

"No. I don't know. Maybe. I'm not sure which box to put you in."

"I'm a rancher, an agriculture specialist and a man of God."

"A man of many boxes."

"A woman with a lot on her mind," he countered.

"Not so much," she replied as she pushed her feet on the ground and set the glider back in motion. "I just have a lot of questions. I'm not sure how I fit here. I'm not at all sure what we're doing, sitting here together. Nothing is the same. Including us."

She had a very valid point. "No, I guess we're not the same," he agreed.

They were different people on different sides of the

faith issue. They still had a huge chasm between them, their past.

He glanced at his watch. "I should go."

"I'm sorry," she said. Her hand touched his arm, just a brief connection, and then she stood.

"It's okay." He reached for her hand and she walked with him to the truck. "I'm here if you ever decide you need someone."

He reached out, brushed a strand of hair behind her ear, then he couldn't seem to move away. Her breath caught and he leaned in, thinking about how good it would feel to pull her close and kiss her the way he used to. But he didn't.

He dropped his hand and backed away.

"Definitely time for me to go," he said.

"Yes, definitely."

He came close to making a clean getaway, but as he reached for the door, another truck came up the drive.

"It's Jake," Samantha said. As if he didn't recognize that big truck and the man behind the wheel.

"When I woke up this morning, I never thought it would be my last day on earth," he half joked.

She laughed, a sweet sound that made him almost glad to be caught by Jake Martin. "I won't let him hurt you."

"I'm holding you to that."

Jake's truck stopped and he got out. His gaze settled on the two of them. Remington couldn't help but feel as if he was in some kind of déjà vu.

"Remington," Jake said as he walked up to them. "Guess I'm not surprised to see you here."

"I followed Sam home. The battery in her truck is bad."

"We'll get that checked tomorrow. Thanks for helping her."

"That's my cue to leave," he said. Man, the Martin ego didn't fade with time.

"I'm not telling you to leave," Jake said without a hint of a smile.

"Right. But I've got to go anyway. My family is waiting for me at Duke's." He ignored Jake and let his gaze settle on Sam. "If you need anything…"

"Thank you," she said with a look that reached deep down, to feelings he thought he'd left behind.

It was all in the past, he told himself. But standing there next to her loosened something inside him, made him wish she was part of his present.

Chapter Six

On Saturday, Samantha hauled Lilly and her horse to the rodeo grounds for the second time that week. She stood inside the arena, watching as her niece brought her horse around the last barrel and headed for the home stretch. The gelding stumbled a bit and Samantha's breath caught and held, her heart thudding painfully, as she watched her niece wobble and fight for control.

And get control. She let out the breath she'd held and shook her head. Lilly didn't give an inch. She kept that gelding on track and brought him on home, reining him in as she passed the finish line.

"You look a little pale, Aunt Sam," the cheeky girl said.

"I think you just shaved a few years off my life. But you did great."

"So what's holding back my time?"

Samantha thought about it, reliving the ride in her mind. "I think you're pulling back a bit after the third barrel. Lean in over his neck and loosen up on the reins. Let's try working on that. Next time."

"But…"

Sam stopped her. "We're not going to wear your horse out."

A truck rattled down the rutted driveway. They both turned to look and Lilly chuckled. "That's trouble with a capital *T*, my dad says."

"Your dad doesn't know everything."

"Dad said he's probably in town to stay and that's rotten timing." Lilly dismounted, landing lightly on the ground next to her gelding, Chief.

"Really? He said that, did he? Anything else I should know?"

Lilly grinned big, managing to look a lot like her dad. "Yeah. He also said at least you're an adult now and not his problem."

Samantha shook her head. "You're incorrigible."

"I looked that up and I know what it means." Lilly grinned. "And I probably am. He's heading this way."

"He doesn't know when to quit," Sam murmured.

Lilly laughed at that. "So he's incorrigible, too."

Samantha groaned. "Go put your horse in the trailer."

"I'm not sure if I'm supposed to leave the two of you alone," Lilly said. She looked from Remington to Sam and back again.

"Lilly, I'm twenty-five and you can leave me alone. Please."

"Fine, but if something happens, it isn't my fault."

Lilly walked off, leading her big red gelding by a chunk of mane. She spoke softly, talking to him as if he was her best friend. The horse nuzzled the girl's dark hair and she laughed. Samantha looked away from the happy pair and focused on the man heading in her direction. Years ago when she would see him in cowboy boots, jeans, a T-shirt and hair damp from the shower, she'd nearly swoon. Her mood would brighten. Her heart would ache with happiness because he loved her.

She'd wanted that love. Desperately. She'd wanted to belong to someone and to know that someone belonged to her. Yes, she'd had her siblings, but they hadn't really been able to give her what she needed. Someone of her own. And he'd been there.

After ten years, she'd learned that no one person could supply what she was looking for or be responsible for her happiness. Happiness had to come from within.

"Saw you from the road," he offered as he drew closer. "I thought I'd see how the lessons are going."

"She's doing great. I think she'll ride next week in the junior division."

"Good for her."

Sam didn't know what else to say. They'd come close to kissing the other night. That wasn't something she wanted to discuss. Even though she had spent a lot of time thinking about it, wondering what it would be like, telling herself it was the wrong path to take.

"I guess I should go check on Lilly," Samantha finally said.

Remington reached for her arm, stopping her. "Sam, would you like to go to Austin with me."

"Austin? With you?" she repeated back to him.

One corner of his mouth tilted up. "Yeah. To Austin. With me. I have to take John Wayne to a group home for foster children. I thought you might like to go with me. I'd like it if you did."

"Do you remember in *The Little Mermaid*," a voice piped up behind them, "when all the sea creatures sing about kissing the girl. You know the song?"

Lilly had reappeared.

"Lilly, I'm warning you," Sam said in a low voice that she hoped sounded authoritative.

Remington laughed. "Lilly, you're my favorite Martin."

She gave him a cheeky grin. "Thank you. You're my favorite problem."

"Enough," Sam warned. She couldn't avoid Remington forever. He was standing there, waiting, smiling. As if he thought they'd just pick up where they left off.

But they couldn't.

"Come with me, Sam." He stepped a little closer, close enough that she could see the flecks of gold in his gray eyes.

"I have to take Lilly and her horse back to the ranch. I have laundry and housework."

"Excuses, excuses." He winked, matching it with a grin. "I never thought you were a chicken."

"I'm not. I'm just very busy."

"Yes, laundry. I heard. Or you could go with me and meet some great kids. It's your choice."

"You're not playing fair."

He laughed. "You're right, I'm not. I'll get John Wayne loaded up and meet you at your place in an hour."

"I'll be ready." She sighed.

An hour later she heard his truck pull up to her house. She pulled on her boots and grabbed her purse. And then she slowly walked out the front door, trying not to seem overeager. He got out and opened the passenger door for her.

Her gaze locked with his. It was easy to get lost in those gray eyes, especially when he was close and his hand touched hers. No. She wanted to say the word, but she didn't. She couldn't.

"Sam?"

If she pulled away, he would let her go. She didn't pull away. Not when he took a step closer. Not when her heart reacted with a painful squeeze.

She closed her eyes. Then common sense returned with a vengeance. She shook her head and backed away.

"No."

Remington let out a breath. "You're right. I know you're right. There was a moment there, though, when it felt…"

She shook her head, cutting him off. "No, don't. We had something ten years ago. We can be friends now but we can't go back to the way it was."

"Why is that?" he asked.

"Because it hurt too much, Rem. It hurt to be sent away. It hurt to be all alone."

"Who says I'm walking away?"

"No one. But who says you're staying?"

He pulled off his hat and ran a hand through his dark hair. "I guess I'm saying that."

"But we've changed. We're older. We should definitely be more mature," she said. "We're in two different places. Spiritually we're worlds apart right now."

"Care to explain?" He said it so easily, as if the balance of their relationship wasn't hinged to the question.

"I shouldn't have to spell it out. You're in ministry. My faith has been eroded. It isn't broken or gone, just badly bruised."

"I've considered that. I know the smart thing to do would be to walk away before either of us gets hurt.

But, Sam, I can't. Not until I know what is or isn't here between us."

"You're not making this easy."

He grinned and reached to open the truck door for her. "I don't plan on making it easy."

The group home in Austin housed fifteen kids of various ages. Several workers were present. Remington led John Wayne around the backyard of the facility. They'd done a few tricks, talked to the children. Now they were socializing. He guessed that was always his favorite part of an event. He loved watching expressions on the children's faces when John did various tricks. They were always in awe of his four-legged partner.

But getting to know the kids, hearing their stories— that was the part he most enjoyed. Sometimes his heart got a little banged up in the process. In the hospitals there were stories of disease, lifelong struggles, hope and fear. In homes such as this one he heard about the worst of humanity. Children who were left to go hungry, were beaten or abandoned.

But now they were safe. They were fed. They were happy. They told stories the way veterans recounted war.

In a quiet moment he looked around, searching for Samantha. He spotted her on a swing, a little girl sitting on her lap. Sam pushed with her feet and the swing moved just the slightest bit, back and forth. The little girl, maybe four years old, looked up at Sam as if she was the best thing ever. He agreed with her.

He headed in their direction, John Wayne trotting obediently at his side. Then suddenly they were stopped. John froze. Remington looked down at the boy who had hurried to catch up with them. He wrapped his arms around John's neck and the horse stood without moving, the boy's thin arms hugging him tight.

"I want a horse like this one," the boy said. "I'd change his name, though."

"Change his name! What else would you call him?"

"I don't know, but I've never heard the name John Wayne and I think he should be called Midnight. Or King."

Remington bit back a grin and tried hard to keep a serious expression on his face.

"Well, John Wayne just happened to be one of the best cowboys ever," he explained. "He was an actor in movies about the Old West."

"Old West?" A girl had walked over to them.

"Yes, ma'am. He played Rooster Cogburn."

They looked at him as if he came from Mars. "But you said he was a cowboy. How'd he play a rooster?" the little boy asked.

Finally Remington laughed. "He didn't play a rooster. That was his name."

"You could have named John Wayne, Rooster," the girl offered.

"Yeah, I guess I could have." He scratched his jaw and kept a serious face. "But then he wouldn't be John Wayne."

"I still like Midnight," the boy said with conviction.

"Midnight is a real good name. I think if I get another horse, that's what I'll name him."

The boy grinned big. "And you'd bring him here so I could see him."

"I'd definitely bring him here to visit."

The girl patted John's neck. "I think John Wayne would like a friend."

"He's got me," Remington offered.

The girl rolled her eyes. "You're a person. He needs horse friends."

Samantha appeared at his side, her new friend still holding tight to her neck. "I agree. John needs horse friends."

"You're not helping," he whispered.

She laughed, and her blue eyes sparkled, but he saw remnants of unshed tears, as if the heartache of the little girl had become her own.

"I'm trying," she said. "Here comes Mrs. Baker."

Mrs. Baker was a widow with a heart for kids. She said this house full of little ones kept her young, kept her heart in the right place. They anchored her.

"Children, it's time to say goodbye to Remington and John Wayne. We have to clean our rooms before dinner," Mrs. Baker announced.

The children groaned and Remington noticed little arms tightening around Sam's neck, holding on for dear life. Mrs. Baker noticed, too, and headed their way.

"I'll take Jalee." Mrs. Baker reached for the little girl who clutched Sam.

"I want to go," Jalee cried. "I want to go."

Samantha closed her eyes as the little girl was pulled away. Her arms slipped to her sides and Remington saw the tear trickle down her cheek. He reached for her hand and she laced her fingers through his. Mrs. Baker gave him an apologetic look.

"Thank you all for coming. I do hope you can come back again."

"We'll make it a regular visit, if that's okay with you." Remington pulled John up to his side.

"We'd love that. I'll give you a call."

She walked away, rounding up the children and herding them inside. The workers helped, taking smaller children by the hands.

"Are you okay?" he asked as they headed for the back gate.

Sam nodded. "I'm good. I just didn't expect that."

"No, of course you didn't."

They reached the driveway where his truck and trailer were parked. He gave her the lead rope for John Wayne as he opened the back of the trailer. Sam led John to him and the little horse stepped right in, heading for hay and water that were always waiting for him at the end of an event.

It didn't take five minutes to put away their props, close up the trailer and head out of town. They were driving when Sam spoke up.

"I'm sorry for being so emotional," she apologized.

He glanced her way and saw that she was looking out the window. "No need to apologize. I get that way, too."

"Do you?"

"Of course. How could a person not get emotional, seeing those kids and hearing their stories?"

"You're a good man, Remington Jenkins. And I'm sure you're a wonderful pastor."

"Thank you. I think that's a compliment."

"It is."

"Then you'll come sometime, to Countryside? I'll let you sit in the front pew and make fun of me."

"Oh, that's tempting."

"But no?"

"Maybe someday. When you're least expecting it."

He drove a little while without talking, then he had to ask. "The little girl, Jalee. She reminded you of yourself?"

There was a long stretch of silence on that long stretch of road.

"Yes," she said. "That little girl reminded me of myself. I know how it feels, to want a mommy to hold on to. A mommy who isn't there. But that little girl has Mrs. Baker. I'm so glad she does."

"Have you considered seeing your mom? Gus said she's in Dallas in a nursing home. Duke found her?"

"Yeah, she's in a home. She has dementia. And of course everyone thinks I need to see her. I need closure. But I don't. I'm fine. I don't need to work through this."

He disagreed, but he wasn't going to tell her. He guessed she probably knew she was wrong. "I would go with you, if you wanted."

"I don't need someone to go with me."

"Okay." He left it alone. He was starting to see a pattern emerging. Sam the invincible, pushing everyone out of her life.

They drove a little farther as he tried to find the best way to break through the walls she'd put up. "What happened, Sam?"

"What?"

"After you left. What happened? I know it hurt because I lived it, too. But why the anger?"

"I'm not angry, Rem. I'm really just…"

"Shut down?"

She shrugged a shoulder. "Maybe. No. I don't know. One day I'm happy and living my life. And the next I'm on a plane to an aunt who decides I need an altogether different life. Even my faith wasn't the right faith. I was a sinful, willful child, who needed to realize that God would probably forgive me, but it was going to take hard work on my part."

"Sam, she was wrong."

"I know," she said, her voice soft. "But it felt as if she was right." She pointed to an abandoned feed store. "You should pull in there."

He didn't question her. He slowed the truck and turned into the dusty, empty parking lot. "Okay, we're here. Why are we here?"

She closed her eyes and drew in a breath. "To talk," she said. "I can't put this off any longer." He knew that this was one of those moments. A moment of truth. And nothing would ever be the same.

Chapter Seven

For years Samantha had thought about how she would tell him. She'd written it down. She'd even prayed a time or two. Yes, she still believed. She just wanted God to be the God she remembered, not the vengeful, angry God that her aunt had introduced her to.

"Sam?"

His voice, familiar but stronger, deeper. She breathed in, wanting to breathe in his scent, his presence. Because after today he would have to work at forgiving her the way she'd been working at forgiving herself.

"When I left town," she started, then she didn't know where to go next. She couldn't remember all of those well-planned speeches she'd written over the years. And saying it was so much harder than writing it down. Saying it out loud would make it all so real.

"I'm here and I'm not going anywhere," he said.

She wished that could be true. "Rem, I was pregnant."

The words were so loud, so harsh. She hadn't planned it that way. She'd planned to ease in, to say it gently. But it was out there between them, cold, harsh and painful. She'd closed her eyes, then opened them and looked at him.

He was staring straight ahead. He was beautiful. He was strong. He couldn't—wouldn't—be able to forgive this.

She wanted to touch him. She reached out to put her hand on his arm, then didn't because sometimes a person had to be alone with their pain, to come to terms with it.

"You were pregnant," he said, the words holding all of the agony she had felt for so long.

"Yes. My aunt homeschooled me throughout the pregnancy. And when I had the baby she arranged the adoption."

"A baby," he said softly. "Where is our baby, Sam?"

"In Tennessee. She lives with a good family. They love her. She's safe."

"It was a girl?"

"Yes. Her name is Marlie. I don't know her last name. But I have pictures. She'll be nine this year."

He held up a hand. "Give me a minute. Right now I'm so angry with you, I can't see straight."

His hands gripped the steering wheel and he leaned back, eyes closed, jaw clenched.

"I'm sorry."

"You didn't think this was something I should know?"

She felt anger roll over her like a wave beating against the shore. "You think I was allowed to make any decisions? I was barely sixteen. I didn't have a say in anything. I didn't have your address or a way to contact you."

"You could have found it. Gus would have gotten word to me."

"Rem, Gus knew. My brothers talked to him. And then they decided my future. They told me it was best for me, for the baby and for you, if I gave her up. After all, you were getting ready to start college. You didn't need this, they said."

"I would have been there for you."

"I wanted you to come and get me. I waited," she admitted. She'd never wanted him to know how desperate she'd been for him.

"We have a daughter." He started the truck and pulled back onto the road. "I have a daughter and I'm never going to have a chance to know her."

"I have pictures and letters from her adoptive family."

He shook his head. "I don't want to see pictures or read letters. Not right now."

"I'm sorry."

"You should have told me. I understand you didn't have a lot of choices, but you haven't been a sixteen-year-old for a long time."

"I know. I've thought and thought about the right way to tell you. But…" There had never really been a right way.

Dusk was settling when he pulled up to her place. The sky was hazy and bees swarmed as she got out of his truck. She stood there with the door open, looking in at him. He had every right to be hurt. She knew his pain, knew it because she'd experienced it ten years ago.

For him, it was fresh and new.

"When you're ready to talk about it," she said, gesturing to the cottage she now called home, "I'm here."

"I'm not sure when I'm going to be ready to talk."

"Okay," she said, backing away from the truck to close the door. She paused, still standing in the opening. "Rem, I hope someday you'll forgive me."

"I'll forgive you, Sam. I just need time to process this. It isn't every day that a man finds out he could have been a father."

She closed the truck door and walked across the lawn, avoiding the house and heading for the barn, to the dog Lady and her puppies. As she watched them together in the stall, she heard a vehicle pull up. She stepped outside, groaning when she saw her brother Brody getting out of his truck.

She was blessed with three brothers, and they all had some say in her life. At least Brody, just a few years older, was easier to deal with.

"Hey, sis," Brody called out as he headed her way.

Her gaze dropped to his uneven walk. He was limping again.

"Hey, Brody. How are you?"

He gave her a long, steady look. "Better than you."

"What's wrong with me?"

"You never could cry pretty like some women. Your face is red and your eyes are puffy. Does this have something to do with Remington Jenkins?"

She shook her head and headed for the house. "No brotherly interference, please."

"Then do you need a shoulder?"

When he got closer, she leaned her head on his shoulder for a few seconds. He gave her an awkward pat, and then hugged her.

"Okay, thank you. Now I'm good." Surprisingly, it did help. "I told him."

"About the baby?"

"Yes. It was never right to keep it from him." She continued walking toward the house, Brody following next to her.

"No, it wasn't. How'd he take it?"

She opened the back door and stepped inside her air-conditioned house. The cool air felt good after the humidity outside.

"As well as expected. I'm sure he'll never speak to me again. And that's fine. We're too old to take up where we left off. Also, he's a little too much like my brothers."

"Hey! What's wrong with your brothers?" he asked.

"They're bossy, overprotective and…" She looked up at him. His cowboy hat was pushed back and his blue eyes were kind. She loved him. "They're the best. But I don't need that. I don't want to go back."

She was ready to move forward. She had a home, a new job and a life and relationships to rebuild in Martin's Crossing.

"I don't blame you. But sometimes our past somehow ends up in our future."

"Just because it happened for you doesn't mean it will happen for me." She loved her brother and his new wife, Grace. That didn't mean she was destined for the same happy ending.

"We all have a story, Sam." He poured himself a glass of tea and headed for the kitchen table.

"Help yourself."

"Don't mind if I do." He eased himself into a chair and waited for her to join him. She worried that his rheumatoid arthritis was flaring, but she wasn't going to ask.

"Okay, you're drinking my tea and sitting at my table. What do you really want?"

He set the glass down on a napkin. "I'm going up to see our mom. I thought you might like to come."

"She isn't my mother. She doesn't know my name. She doesn't even remember leaving me. I was a baby, Brody."

She blinked quickly because she wasn't going to cry over Sylvia Martin and what she'd done to them all of those years ago, leaving without looking back. Never caring what happened to her children after she left town. Having another child with another man and abandoning her with her own father. Kayla Stanford lived in Austin. Samantha had developed a growing relationship with her sister, but sisters shouldn't have to get to know one another. They should have always had each other.

"Sam, don't do it for her. Do it for yourself."

"Why?"

"Because forgiving her would help you get past it," he said in the same soothing tones he used on an unbroke horse.

"No."

"I'm going up there in two weeks. I'd like you to think about it."

He was the most forgiving man she knew. He'd forgiven Grace for walking away from him. He'd forgiven their mother. She wanted a little of his ability to let go.

"I'll think about it."

"That's all I'm asking." He finished the rest of his tea and carried the glass to the sink. "Marty made a big roast. More than we could possibly eat. Do you want to come down? Bria is asking for you."

"My four-month-old niece is asking for me?" She smiled at that.

"Well, she did coo something that sounded like Aunt Sam."

She started to tell him no. That was her typical answer when pushed by her brothers to join them. But today the thought of spending time with Bria, holding her, listening to her sweet laugh, was appealing.

Spending time with Brody and his family would keep her mind off Remington. It would help her deal with the huge chunk of her heart that seemed to be missing.

After dropping Sam off at her place, Remington headed home. When he got back to the Rocking J, he traded his truck for the farm truck. He checked the toolbox in the back for the supplies he needed and headed for the field. He needed to pound something, and he figured fixing fence would do the trick.

He had a daughter. But he didn't. His mind wouldn't calm down. He wanted to know her. What color was her hair? Did she have his gray eyes, or Sam's blue eyes? Did she laugh the way Sam laughed, all out, nothing held back? Did she have a good life? Was she loved?

When he reached the section of fence he knew needed serious attention, he stopped the truck. The fence sagged and most of the posts leaned. What the place needed was new fencing. A lot of new fencing. But repairs would have to be enough for now. He got out and headed for the toolbox on the back of the flatbed. He dug out gloves and the tools he would need. He'd brought a few new posts to replace the ones that were bent or missing.

The ranch had gone downhill in the past couple of

years. The family figured Gus had been having mini-strokes for a while before the stroke that hospitalized him this past winter. Remington's grandfather's poor health was the only explanation for these deteriorating conditions. The fences, the barns, even the cattle—everything needed attention. Remington had worked for the State Department of Agriculture, but he'd left the job because this place, Martin's Crossing, the church and helping his grandfather, all felt right. It fit him better than a government job.

He pulled on his gloves and tackled the fence. The loose fence posts needed to be reset. He went to work, pounding them firmly back into the soil. The sun had started to sink on the horizon and the air cooled somewhat. He pounded fence posts until his muscles ached and perspiration trickled down his back.

With each strike he tried to force away the anger brewing inside him. He should have known he had a daughter. Someone should have told him.

He'd lost her before he'd ever had her. He tossed the fence-post driver to the ground and brushed a gloved hand across his face. He was stretching barbed wire to reattach it to the post when the sound of a vehicle heading his way caught his attention. He clamped the wire, attaching it to the post, and turned to watch Gus pull up. Remington pulled off his hat and took a deep breath. Cool wind blew across the field, bringing a hint of rain in the air.

Gus got out, surveyed the fence, studied Remington, then tugged on his bushy gray mustache. Bowlegged with his jeans hanging loose, Gus headed his way. "Thought I might ought to check on you."

"Did you?" Remington picked up the tools and tossed

them into the box on the back of the truck. He'd have to finish Monday. By then the rain would have blown over, some of his anger with it. Gus approached, his left leg seeming to drag just a bit.

"Yes, I did," Gus said. "I didn't expect to find you as surly as an old bear. What's the matter?"

Remington took a deep breath and said a prayer. He didn't want to lose his temper, not with his grandfather. Gus might be a bit misguided, but he was good as gold and always did what he felt was right. Taking in his sister and her grandson was one of those right things.

"I'm a little bit angry." Remington sat down on the back of the truck. Gus leaned against it, not bothering to try to take a seat.

"I thought you were in Austin at a group home? So what's got you all worked up?"

"Sam came with me. On the way home I got some unexpected news." Remington brushed a hand through his hair and avoided looking at Gus. "I found out I had a daughter."

Had. Not have. Past tense. And it riled him all over again.

Gus stood there silent, his hand tugging on his mustache, his face shadowed by his wide-brimmed hat. Finally he nodded. "She told you."

"Yeah, she told me. I should have known sooner. I should have known when it happened."

"What would you have done differently? She was sixteen and you were just starting college. You were both too young. You made a mistake. And it would have been a bigger mistake for the two of you to settle down as parents."

"Shouldn't that have been my decision to make?"

Remington said the words quietly, but man, he wanted to shout. He wanted to give in to temper and outrage. To pain. "How did you all decide that I couldn't man up and be a father and husband?"

"Guess we just made a decision, Rem. It felt like the right thing to do. And I can't say that I'd do it any differently."

Remington shook his head. "At some point you could have told me."

"I guess I could have," the older man sighed. "But time has a way of getting away from us. We think we'll do something, and then time goes by, and then it seems like it might be best to let it go."

"It was my baby, Gus."

Gus rested a hand on Remington's arm. "I know that and I'm sorry."

Remington nodded, pretending he didn't feel a little dampness in his eyes. He watched as cattle in the distance moved toward the pond. The clouds overhead dropped a few fat raindrops and thunder rumbled across the hills. "I guess we should head in."

"Did you manage to pound those fence posts to death?" Gus asked.

A grin eased the tension inside Remington. "Yeah, I guess I did. Tomorrow I'll come back and do this up right. Today I just needed to take out some frustration."

"How's things stand between you and Sam?"

"Probably not the best." Remington admitted. "Not that it matters."

Gus studied him for a long, uncomfortable minute. "You sure about that?"

"I'm not sure about much of anything right now. I

do know that the past is just the past. It's been lived and it's long gone."

Gus headed for his truck, grumbling about fool, stubborn kids. Remington saw him hesitate when he got to the truck. He watched him stiffen and reach for the door handle.

"Gus?"

He got no response, and a trickle of fear edged through him.

"Gus, you okay?" Remington headed for his granddad. Before he could reach him, Gus turned, his face a little pale.

"I'm good. Probably just my blood sugar. Doc says I have to watch what I eat. Some foolishness about potatoes and bread being sugar. I don't get that. I put…I put…" He shook his head. "Sugar. I put sugar in my coffee. Not potatoes."

With that, Gus climbed in the truck, started it and headed off across the field.

When Remington got to the house after putting up the farm truck and checking on John Wayne, Gus had gone to bed. He'd told Aunt Lee his blood sugar levels were high and he'd just go to bed early and sleep off those potatoes and bread.

Aunt Lee repeated the explanation as she finished washing dishes. "But Rem, he looked pale and seemed confused."

"He had some kind of spell back in the field." Remington thought about the angry words he'd shared with his grandfather. "We argued."

"That doesn't mean anything. He's not as healthy as he likes to pretend." She dried her hands and offered him a sympathetic look. "He's also stubborn. He's my brother and I love him, but he won't take a break for anything."

"No, he won't."

Parker pushed himself into the room. He had a big grin on his face.

"What are you up to?" Remington asked, eyeing his little cousin.

"Nothing. I just...well, nothing."

"Nothing?" Aunt Lee asked.

He shook his head.

"Still getting baptized tomorrow?" Remington asked as he poured himself a glass of milk and grabbed one of the cookies his aunt had made.

"Yeah," Parker said, eyeing the cookie. "I'm ready."

They had talked at length about this step of faith. Remington wouldn't have agreed if he hadn't known that the boy was ready. Parker was nine, almost ten; sometimes he seemed to be closer to fifty.

"Could I have another cookie?" Parker asked, giving his grandmother a sweet look that had her laughing.

Remington took his milk and cookie with him as he walked away, leaving Aunt Lee and her grandson. The two of them had been through a lot but they were surviving, together. His thoughts went back to Samantha Martin. He didn't know how to feel about her. Angry?

Connected?

The word took him by surprise. He'd managed to work through most of his anger, taking it out on the fence posts he'd pounded into the ground. They might have had a connection, but after today he wasn't sure that what they shared would survive.

He and Samantha had a daughter. That was a lot for a man to just let go of.

Chapter Eight

Countryside Church had been built decades ago. Today it stood as a sentinel of the past, a brick-sided building on a country road. Two dozen or so cars filled the gravel parking lot.

Church was the last place Samantha wanted to be, but when Parker called the previous evening, she hadn't been able to tell him no. He was getting baptized today. She wanted to see that, to be there for him. And what could she have said? That because her aunt had hurt her, she avoided church like the plague?

Besides, this wasn't Aunt Mavis's church.

And she knew she would have to eventually face Remington. She would have to look him in the eyes, knowing he resented her, and he had good reason. Maybe that resentment would help them to keep their priorities straight and not get pulled back into anything.

As she walked through the doors of the little country church, she stopped and took in her surroundings. The sanctuary was bathed in golden, early-morning light. It not only felt peaceful, it looked peaceful. She drew in a deep breath of air that smelled like furniture polish, sunshine and age.

What did sunshine smell like? Warmth? Lemons? Maybe spring and good soaking rains.

"Imagine seeing you here."

She opened her eyes, smiling at Remington before she realized she was smiling. He stood before her, a slightly more polished version of the cowboy she knew. He wore a button-up shirt and crisp, dark jeans. His boots were polished, not the ones he wore to work in. His dark hair curled just slightly without a cowboy hat to flatten it down.

"I was invited," she said with clipped words she hadn't intended.

"I assumed you were," Remington answered. "But you don't have to be invited, you know."

"No, of course not." She let the words trail off as she looked up, into the unsettling gray of his eyes. What did she do or say now?

"I'll walk with you," he offered. "I figure you'll want to sit with Gus, Lee and Parker."

"Yes, of course, but you don't have to do this, you know."

"What? Walk with you? Forgive you?"

"All of the above."

He shrugged it off, as if it didn't matter. But deep in his eyes, she could see that it did.

"I'm good."

She let it go because this wasn't the time or the place to push. She let him walk her down the aisle, and then she nearly choked on the thought. There they were, walking down the aisle, dozens of curious onlookers and no way out.

"Well, this is uncomfortable." She giggled as she said it.

Remington glanced down at her. "You always do find the amusement in the strangest things."

"You're walking me down the aisle."

His smile faltered briefly. "I would have, you know."

"Don't," she said too quickly. "Let me joke and smile right now. And maybe, when you can, forgive me."

He didn't get a chance to respond. Parker was suddenly in front of her. His grandmother sat on the pew behind him and next to her sat Gus. She gave the older man a careful look, concerned by the slightest drooping of his left eye.

"Good morning." She leaned to hug Remington's aunt Lee, then she touched Parker's shoulder.

"Parker. Thank you for inviting me," Sam said, choking up a little.

He grinned big. "You're like our family."

"And I wouldn't miss this for anything." She took a seat next to his grandmother. Her attention again strayed to Gus. She started to ask him how he was doing, but she didn't get a chance.

Piano music, a little loud and not well played, filled the sanctuary of the old church. Samantha glanced toward the tiny stage area, past the pulpit and past the poor man trying to lead the singing. The pianist, gray haired with wire-framed glasses perched on her nose, smiled joyfully and continued to bang away at the keys.

Samantha made the mistake of looking at Parker. His eyes sparkled and he bit down on his bottom lip. Okay, she couldn't look at the nine-year-old. She glanced toward the front of the church, where Remington sat alone in a chair and she noticed he had closed his eyes.

All around her, people tried to sing along to the discordant but rapturous music. But no one laughed. They all sang along to "I'll Fly Away." The piano had so overwhelmed her she hadn't quite noticed, but now that she recognized the song she tried to sing along. She stood with the rest of the congregation and made the best of what appeared to be the worst pianist in history.

But no one seemed to care. They sang hymn after hymn with music that rocked the little church. No matter how bad the pianist, the words of those songs still meant the same thing.

There was faith in difficult times. There was hope. There was a light. Samantha tried to shut down as she'd done so many times in her aunt Mavis's church. But in this church she couldn't tune out the message. She couldn't pretend she didn't need hope.

Everyone needed hope. But some felt less deserving.

If it hadn't been for Parker, she would have slipped quietly away. She stayed.

Parker was counting on her. She felt his hand on her arm, and she gave him a look that she hoped was reassuring. He blinked quickly because he was nine and he wasn't going to cry like a baby. He'd told her that once in the hospital, and she'd told him she was twenty-five and if she were him, she would cry. He hadn't given in. He'd shaken his head and told her no, he wouldn't cry.

"You okay?" she whispered.

Parker nodded but didn't speak. She guessed if he spoke he might lose the tight control he had on his emotions.

"They're watching from heaven," she said, guessing where his thoughts were headed. "And they're proud."

"People don't watch from heaven," he choked out. "Didn't you hear the song? Everybody will be happy over there. They can't be happy if they look down."

"Oh, buddy." She closed her eyes and drew in a breath. "I'm sorry."

"Don't cry," he warned. His voice was small and quiet. "Don't cry." More to himself than to her.

Then Remington stood in front of them, a smile on his too-handsome face and eyes that showed understanding and warmth. "Ready?"

Parker nodded. "Can Sam go with me?"

"She can if she wants."

How could she say no? She would share this moment with him. She would walk next to Remington and with his aunt Lee. They made their way to the baptismal with a little boy who wanted his faith to be made public. It was a ceremony as old as time. Not a dry eye remained in the church as Remington baptized his cousin.

The pianist suddenly sat straight up, raised her hands and began to beat out a worthy tempo on that poor old upright piano. She grinned broadly, her glasses sliding to the end of her nose. She paused to push them back up, and then she went back to playing.

Remington stepped close to Samantha, Parker in his arms. "And that's how we have church in the country."

"Will you join us for lunch?" Parker's grandmother asked as they left the church a short time later.

"I'd love to but I have to go to work. Another time?"

"When are you scheduled to come to the house again?" Parker asked.

She'd thought about it, that someone else should take over his case. But she couldn't walk away from Parker. As much as it hurt to be around Remington. As much as she had hurt him, they couldn't avoid each other. Parker came first.

Remington took his family to Duke's No Bar and Grill for lunch that Sunday. Why not poke the bear? The bear being Duke Martin.

Duke didn't seem too upset to see him. The middle Martin brother, Duke was the tallest and probably the most dangerous of the bunch. As Remington and his small family took their seats, Duke left the table where he'd been having lunch with the Martin clan. And they were quite a big group these days.

"Remington, good to have you all with us. Might as well join the Martins. We have a big table at the back." Duke pointed in the direction of three tables pushed together. "Marty had the day off. She's busy dating and it looks like we might lose her to a worthy adversary, Oregon's dad, Joe."

"Well, I'll be," Gus said. "I watched television."

At that non sequitur, Remington glanced at his granddad. "Gus, you okay?"

"Why wouldn't I be? I'm happy for Marty and Joe. Both good people."

"You said you watch television." Remington glanced at Aunt Lee. She glanced from Remington to Gus and shook her head.

"Well, I don't know but I know what I meant to say. Let's join this crew for lunch."

"Gus, we should go to the hospital." Remington pulled his grandfather aside. "You've been doing this for a few days and I've let it go. I shouldn't have, but I did."

Gus shook his head. "Don't be a bother, boy."

"I'm not being a bother. I'm being someone who cares enough to let you be angry with me when I insist on taking you to the hospital."

"We can feed Lee and Parker," Duke offered. "Then give them a ride home."

Gus headed for the door, grumbling that he was old enough to know when he needed medical help. Remington looked to his aunt and she nodded.

"Take him. I can't lose my brother on top of…" She stopped herself, glancing around to make sure Parker had moved away. The boy was at the table with the Martins, acting as if he'd been in their lives forever. He and Lilly Martin were having a conversation that included a lot of hand gestures.

"Don't worry. I'm sure he's fine," Remington assured his aunt. "I'll call you."

"Where are we going?" Gus asked as Remington got behind the wheel of the truck a few minutes later.

"Braswell is closer than anywhere else."

"Fool-headed boy. I'm fine."

Remington headed out of town in the direction of Braswell.

"Gus, you're not fine. For the second time in two days you've had a spell."

"It's because I've been eating too much sugar."

"That could be, Gus, but we're going to find out for sure." Remington picked up his phone and dialed his parents. They were on vacation in California, but he knew they'd want to be informed.

"I don't know why you're calling them," Gus snarled.

The phone went to voice mail and he left a message. After he'd hung up he glanced at Gus. His grandfather was slouched down in his seat, his cowboy hat pulled low and a frown on his face.

"Gus."

"Don't tell me what you think I ought to do. You've got no idea, boy. You don't have a clue how it feels to get old. When you were ten, I took you to the doctor because you cut your knee open. I took care of you. I took care of your dad. And now you all think I'm a helpless old man."

"We all take care of each other," Remington offered. He knew it wouldn't make things easier.

"Yeah, I guess we do. I can tell you this, before I head for the other side, I'm going to see that you make things right with that little gal."

"What? Where did that come from?"

Gus shrugged and hunkered down in his seat. "It wasn't a stroke talking. It needed to be said. You're stubborn. You get that from your mom's side."

"Right. Since you brought it up, there's nothing to make right."

Gus tugged on his mustache. "I reckon there is. The two of you have things to work out, and then you'll figure out what the next step is."

"There's no next step. How did we get from your health to Samantha Martin?"

"Because I didn't want to talk about getting older and needing you to take care of me," Gus grumbled, looking out the window.

Remington pulled into the parking lot of the hospital emergency room.

"I'd rather you give me a beating than take me in there where some young doctor is going to talk to me like I'm five and can't answer the questions he's got. 'Mr. Jenkins, when was the last time you had a...'" Gus cleared his throat. "You know."

"Yeah, I know." Remington laughed a little. "You might try to make it easy for them."

"When they ask the questions that no grown man ought to have to answer? No, sir. And if he looks at you, like you can answer and I can't, that's when I'm walking out of this place," Gus said as they walked through the front door.

"If you can walk on your own two feet, more power

to you. And since you're the man in charge, tell this nice receptionist why we're here."

Gus gave the receptionist a charming smile followed by a wink and a tug on that mustache.

"Young lady, my grandson here can't seem to get a date on his own so he wanted me to pretend to be elderly and tell you that I can't seem to form a sentence."

"Gus," Remington warned.

"My grandson thinks I've had some kind of attack."

The receptionist asked a few more questions, and then directed them to a room down the hall. Within minutes they were joined by a nurse and then a doctor. There were questions about the symptoms of Gus's attack, about his state of mind afterward. The doctor explained that he wanted to do tests and that he might possibly admit Gus overnight just to observe him. Two TIAs in two days wasn't something they wanted to ignore.

"Do you think they might feed me some lunch in this place?" Gus asked as they placed an IV. "My grandson didn't even let me eat lunch."

"Mr. Jenkins, we'll get you something to eat," a nurse soothed. "Let's get you settled and we'll have some broth."

Gus held up a hand. "I've got a hankering for chicken and I want it fried, not boiled and all the good stuff taken out."

Remington sighed.

The nurse offered him a sympathetic look. "It's okay. We're used to this behavior. It might seem as if your grandfather isn't acting himself but that can be a symptom of a TIA. You understand TIA, don't you, Mr. Jenkins? Transient Ischemic Attack. It can be a precursor to a stroke, so we do want to take all necessary precautions."

Gus groaned. "I told you they'd talk to me like I'm five and you're the adult."

"Gus, you aren't exactly being pleasant. Or mature."

"Well, you try getting stuck with a needle, being wrapped up in a paper gown with no back and see how pleasant you are. And I didn't get lunch. My blood sugar levels haven't been right, you know that."

"I'm going to get out of here so they can do the tests. I'll be in the waiting room."

"You'll probably be at the cafeteria having fried chicken," Gus called out to him as he left the room.

Remington highly doubted the hospital cafeteria had fried chicken.

When he got to the cafeteria, he found they did have a decent grilled fish. He ordered it and headed for a table at the back of the cafeteria. His phone rang as he sat down. It was his dad calling for an update. He filled them in, told them he didn't think they needed to fly home, then he dug into the surprisingly edible lunch.

When a tray plopped down across from his, he looked up. Sam glanced at the empty seat. "Mind if I join you?"

"Of course you can." His good Texas manners kicked in. He got up and pulled the chair out for her. She shot him a look over her shoulder, but she sat down anyway.

"How's Gus doing?" she asked as she cut up her baked chicken.

"How'd you know?"

"Duke called. He told me I might see you here."

"He called to warn you?"

She rolled her eyes. "No, he was worried about Gus."

"Gus is okay. Well enough to argue and grumble."

He watched as she kept her head down as she tackled the chicken on her tray without seeming to really enjoy it. "Bad day on the children's side?"

She nodded and kept eating. One tear trickled down her cheek and she swiped it away. "I'm not sure if I'm cut out for this job."

"It can't be easy."

"It isn't." She pushed aside her tray. "Rem, I'd like to share the letters and pictures with you."

"Someday. Not yet." He didn't even know why not. He guessed he needed more time to come to terms with the fact that he had this daughter out there somewhere. What if they crossed paths someday and didn't know it?

"Okay. When you're ready."

On to lighter topics. "How did you like church?"

One side of her mouth kicked up and her eyes lost the shimmer of sadness. "I enjoyed it."

"And Pearl?"

"Would that be the pianist?"

He laughed at the term *pianist*. "Well, you could call her that. She's eighty-six and she's a gem. She can't play a lick, but she thinks she can. And since no one else knows how, she's our gal."

"I think she's wonderful," Samantha said. He thought from her tone she meant it.

Sitting there across from him, she licked the chocolate off the top of a pudding cup. Her blond hair was pulled back with a headband, and she wore pink scrubs with teddy bears. If she had been any other woman, he might have asked her out.

If he hadn't been angry, still coming to terms with the news she'd given him the other day, he might have admitted to her, and to himself, that he still missed her. He hadn't realized it until she was back in his life.

He couldn't say why she had this effect on him. But he also couldn't lie to himself. Samantha Martin mattered to him.

And that was a complication he doubted he needed.

"Why this job, Sam? Why nursing?" he asked as he finished up the fish.

She looked up from her plate. "I'm not sure. In high school I did a couple of semesters volunteering at a local hospital. My guidance counselor thought it would be good for me to connect and she said it would look good on college applications. So I did my time as a volunteer and I enjoyed it. When I got to college and it was time to pick a major, I picked nursing. I also studied physical therapy and psychology. I was something of a professional student for a few years. I graduated six months ago, worked in Austin for a while, and then came to Braswell."

"You were in Austin?" he said, not sure why that hit him like a ton of bricks.

"For a few months." She closed her eyes. "I should have called. I know I should have."

"But you didn't." He let it go and stood up. "I need to get back to Gus."

"Remington—" she looked up at him "—I really am sorry."

"I know." As much as he wanted to hold on to his anger for a little while longer, he felt it slipping away.

They'd both been hurt. He didn't see a reason to keep holding on to the past or the pain.

They had a present to worry about and that had pushed the two of them into each other's lives. He guessed it was up to them to find a way to be friends and continue taking care of the people counting on them.

Chapter Nine

The sun was barely up when Samantha crawled out of bed Monday morning. She wanted to work with her horse and get some cleaning done before she headed in for her evening work shift. When she strode out the back door, she was surprised to see her brother Jake walking out of her barn.

"What are you doing here?" she asked as she headed his way, her favorite coffee mug in her hand.

"I thought I'd saddle up that new horse of yours."

She held up her free hand. "Stop. Right. There. My horse. My saddle."

"But he's green and you don't ride as much as you used to."

She wanted to ask him whose fault that was, but she didn't.

"Jake, I can saddle my own horse. I can ride my own horse. As a matter of fact I plan on riding him Saturday."

"You think he's ready for that?"

"Only one way to find out." She found that he had indeed already saddled her horse. Buzz was in the barn, cross-tied in the center aisle. "How long have you been here?"

"Thirty minutes. I fed your dog, too."

She peeked in at Lady. "I'm not sure what to say other than, don't you have a wife and kids to take care of?"

"I do, but my wife is of the mind that my younger sister might need some attention."

"Smothering the wife, huh?" Samantha opened the door and stepped in with the dog and her puppies. Lady loved her stall, but she'd been getting out more, traipsing around the yard, sometimes playing at chasing a rabbit or squirrel up a tree. The puppies had their eyes open and were playing in the straw she'd put down for them.

"I'm not smothering my wife. But she did say she needed a break because I was hovering."

Sam laughed. "I could watch the twins and sweet little Irene so the two of you could go out."

Jake rubbed at his chin. "Now that's a great idea. I could surprise…"

She cut him off. "Do *not* surprise Breezy. I don't think she'd appreciate it. She had a baby that she can't stand being away from. Dinner, Jake, not a weekend away."

"No, of course not." He stood on the other side of the stall door. "You're right—you're not a kid. Still my kid sister, but I'm willing to admit that you're an adult. And one that I admire."

"Thank you, big brother."

He grinned. "But I still get to worry from time to time."

"I can let you do that."

He was used to worrying about them. Tall and handsome, he'd had to fight his own battles with their childhood. Breezy had broken down his walls and built the two of them a sweet place together.

Love and romance had been working itself through the hearts of her brothers for the past couple of years. Samantha had enjoyed watching them change, watching them let go. That didn't mean she was interested in the same fall. She was free now. She had her own place. She had her own job and her own life.

And she was horribly jealous. Not that she would admit it. They were all finding happiness, leaving her behind. She'd always felt just outside their circle, and now she felt that distance even more.

"Duke said Lilly showed him last night how she'd improved on Chief," Jake said, watching her closely. "She said it was because you've been helping her."

She gave Lady one last pat on the head and stepped out of the stall. "She's a great kid. She just needed a little help."

"She is great."

Samantha found a brush and walked up to her horse, running her hand down his neck and back, calming him. He was a little green, but he'd come around. She loved his spirit and the sweetness in his eyes. Sweet but with a little fire. She brushed the horse's buttery gold coat and waited for Jake to get to the real reason for his visit.

"Have you heard anything on Gus?"

"No, I don't have an update," she answered as she ran a comb through the horse's tail, patting him on the rump and talking to him so he would know it was her positioned near his back leg. She'd been kicked once as a young teen and she'd become extracautious after that experience.

The horse stomped his foot to rid himself of a fly, and then swished his tail. She finished his tail and moved back to his neck, glancing at Jake as she dropped the brushes in the bucket.

"I haven't heard anything since yesterday. They were watching him but other than that, it was just about running tests and adjusting his meds."

"He's a tough guy. I'm sure he'll be fine."

Samantha untied her horse and held the reins. "Jake, why are you really here?"

"We haven't had a chance to talk in a while."

"I see, and you're worried about me? I'm not fragile. I'm not going to get caught in the barn with Remington Jenkins again. I can't think of anything else that would have you so concerned."

"I don't think you're fragile. I'm also not worried about you and Rem. I know your job is tough. Oregon said you've got a little boy at the hospital who isn't doing well."

That was an understatement. And why in the world did her brother repeating what she knew make her want to cry? She drew in a deep breath and shrugged a shoulder. "It's part of the job."

Jake's blue eyes filled with sympathy. "I'm sorry."

She raised a hand. "Jake, please. I'm good. I can't say that it's easy. It's actually horrible. It's the worst thing I can imagine about my job. But it is my job and I wouldn't trade it for anything."

"Gotcha. But if you need anything…"

She nodded, conceding a small bit of herself to his brotherly strength. "I'll call."

"I'll go. And if you do hear anything about Gus, let me know."

"I'm not going to hear about Gus until I get to work. But I'll text you."

An hour later, Samantha rode Buzz across the field at a pace that would have had her brother sweating bullets. She didn't care. The horse loved it and so did she. They loved the wind. They loved the earth beneath pounding hooves. As she headed back to the barn, she saw a dark blue king cab truck pulled up to her house.

She pulled in the reins a bit and the gelding slowed. But he wasn't happy about it. He pushed, trying to take the bit between his teeth. She kept him in hand and talked to him, soothing his ruffled feathers. He bunny hopped rather than settling into a nice easy trot. The motion was jarring and meant she had to keep him in hand because he would have bolted given half a chance.

She rode into the corral and dropped to the ground next to the horse. Remington was leaning over the fence, watching.

"Rem, I didn't expect you this morning." Or any morning. "How's Gus?"

"He's mad, but he's doing okay. They want to keep him another day and run more tests."

She cringed, thinking of Gus in the hospital. The poor nurses on that floor. They'd have their hands full. But that only distracted her for a moment, then it was back to reality, to Remington.

She led her horse through the door and into the barn. Remington met her inside.

"I want to see the pictures."

She clipped a lead rope to Buzz's halter, then answered him. "Oh. Okay. Let me put Buzz back in the field and we'll go inside."

As she unsaddled and then brushed the horse down, Remington stood to the side watching. She tried to ignore him but couldn't't. He leaned against a stall, studying her as she took care of her horse. His gray eyes were intense, the line of his mouth unsmiling and stern.

She led the horse to the rear door and turned him out to pasture. Remington grabbed her saddle and put it on the stand in the tack room. He hung the bridle and put away the brushes. All without speaking.

"Ready?" he asked as he closed the door to the tack room.

As she would ever be. "Yes," she answered.

She led him across the yard to the back door of the house. When she reached to open the door, his arm shot out, pulling it open for her. She said thank-you, but she didn't know if he heard. It was difficult to push the words past the tight lump in her throat.

She flipped on a light in the kitchen, more out of habit than necessity. Sunlight poured through the windows, adding its own light and warmth. Remington stood just inside the door, unmoving, unsmiling.

She didn't know what to do so she poured them each a glass of tea. Remington moved to the table in the center of the room. He pulled out two chairs and took the glass of tea she held out to him.

"Have a seat. I'll get the box."

He nodded, and she watched him sit down. They used to be more than this, more than two strangers who didn't quite know what to say to one another and didn't easily fit into each other's lives.

That was then, she thought. *This is now.*

Remington waited at the kitchen table while Samantha went to her room to rummage around for pictures. He heard several thumps, then some muttering. He chuckled as he listened. That took him by surprise because he hadn't been too happy with her since she'd told him about their daughter.

He was still coming to terms with the news and still trying to decide how he felt about Samantha. When he'd first met up with her at the hospital, he'd thought maybe this was their second chance. And then obstacles had piled up. Church, his ministry and now the daughter she'd been forced to give up. *His* daughter.

When she returned, he stood and took the box from her hands. He brushed a cobweb from her pale blond hair and his heart pretty near caught fire at the way her hair felt and the catch of her breath when he touched her. He hadn't expected that, not when he'd spent the past few days being about the angriest he'd been in his life. He swiped the cobweb on his jeans and took a careful step back, away from danger.

"I think there's another box but I'm not sure where it is." She took a seat. "I'll find it. Maybe at Jake's."

He sat across from her, the box on the table in front of him. For all intents and purposes he was about to meet his daughter. He rested a hand on the box, not quite ready to delve into the contents.

Sam was watching him, her blue gaze steady but a little apprehensive, if he had to guess. Anger got tangled up with admiration, the two emotions seeming completely at odds. She'd gone through a lot and she'd done it alone. She'd been a kid and she'd handled the hard stuff. Yeah, he admired that.

It would be easy to get caught up in what should have or could have been. None of that really mattered now.

"Well?" she asked.

He opened the box. She sat in her chair, her teeth sinking into those cotton-candy lips that had always distracted him. He let himself be distracted for a moment. It was easier than pulling pictures and letters from the box. Her breath trembled and he knew he wasn't doing much better.

He pulled out the small packet inside and instantly saw himself in the little girl who looked up at him from the picture on the top of the stack. She had dark hair and blue eyes. Her chin. She had Samantha's chin. She had his nose with the slightest bump. His mom said it came from their Native American ancestors.

He kept sifting through the papers and photos, finding more. There were pictures of a baby with a sweet grin, and pictures of the first day in kindergarten. He lifted a letter and read about first words and first steps.

The letters were written by a woman who said she was a teacher in an elementary school. Her husband was a doctor. They lived in a small town. They loved their baby girl.

His baby girl. His and Samantha's. This lady called her daughter a gift, an answer to prayer.

He and Sam had made a mistake. They'd rushed into a relationship unguided and unsupervised. They'd felt all kinds of love. But now he could look back and say with certainty it had been all kinds of teenage hormones.

It had taught him a lesson, that summer. One he'd taken to heart. He no longer rushed. He no longer took chances. He gave respect, because he hadn't shown Sam the respect she deserved.

After looking at the pictures a few more times, he put them away and he looked at the woman sitting across from him, dry-eyed but a little bit lost.

"She's beautiful. Like you."

She shook her head. "Don't. Not right now. Please."

"Right. I'm sorry. You did good, Sam."

"Sometimes I think that. Sometimes it feels like the worst thing ever. But I always come back to good."

"Do you think she'll ever want to meet us?" He'd been thinking about that a lot. In nine years she'd be eighteen.

"I don't know. I promised I would never look for her. But they will give her our information if she should ever want to find us. But even if she wants to meet us, I know I won't ever be her mother. She's been raised by people who love and cherish her. They're her parents. I get Christmas cards and photos to update my album. I'm really okay with that."

"You gave her life. That's a gift. And you gave them a child they couldn't have."

"Okay, let's stop now. I'm not a hero. They left me empty armed and crying in that hospital. I wasn't thinking about the great gift I'd given a childless couple. I was thinking that everyone in my life had let me down and left me alone. I was thinking some very mean things about you. I would have changed my mind. If they'd given me half a chance I would have told them to bring her back. But then, of course, she would have been raised by a teenage girl who no more knew how to be a mom than she knew how to be a lion tamer."

"And now?"

"Now I know that she has a beautiful life and I'm okay with what I did. Are you okay with it?"

"Yes, I am." He didn't hesitate. After seeing the pictures and reading the letters, he truly was.

She let out a shaky breath. "Thank you."

They sat in silence for a long time with that box between them. "I should go. Gus is going to be released this afternoon. Or he hopes he is."

She laughed a little. "The nurses were beside themselves last night. He charmed them, and then he growled, wanting to go home."

"I'm surprised he didn't convince one of them to give him a ride back to Martin's Crossing."

"I went down to see him last night," Sam told him. "He tried to bargain with me. If I'd take him home."

She didn't finish and he could guess some of the things Gus offered. Land. Cattle. Remington.

"That's Gus. He never misses an opportunity."

"No, he doesn't." She moved her hands across the top of the box and he watched, somehow mesmerized by that gesture.

Common sense told him he should go. So he got up from the table, fully intending to make a clean break of it.

"Let's go out to dinner." Where had that come from? So much for a clean break.

"You and me?" One side of her mouth lifted in a smile.

"Why not?" He guessed this was where he got shot down.

"Because there are things that shouldn't be revisited. A few years ago I found my best friend from grade school. Talia. She lives in San Antonio now. I thought we could get together and talk about our childhood, our friendship. We'd been best friends for years. And now, as adults, we have nothing in common. She works in the fashion industry. Her husband works in banking. She doesn't remember swimming in the creek and the snapping turtle that almost got her foot. I don't remember painting jewelry in her bedroom. We've moved on. It was uncomfortable to realize we no longer had a friendship."

"I'm not asking to be your best friend or to read your diary," he said.

Together they walked to the door. Her hand reached for his. He took it, and then pulled her close.

"I know you're not," she said, her mouth dangerously close to his. "We can't go back."

"I agree, Sam, there's no going back. And who would want to? I'm not asking you to go back. I want to move forward. I'm asking if we can see who we are now."

He leaned down and brushed his mouth against hers. She didn't pull away. Instead her arms wrapped loosely around his neck. He softened the kiss, hovering over her lips, and then brushing across her cheek. She sighed, and he pulled her close so that her head rested on his shoulder.

"I don't want to go back, Rem. I don't want that pain all over again. I don't want to miss you again. I don't want to make mistakes that can't be undone."

"I know," he said, kissing the top of her head. "I know."

She pulled back. "I don't want to be the person who can't live up to your expectations."

It should have been easy to tell her that this time they wouldn't make mistakes. This time they'd do everything right and they wouldn't hurt each other. What if he was wrong? What if they went down this road and found out they were two different people who wanted different things?

Chapter Ten

The alarm for room 212 went off as Samantha sat behind the desk finishing paperwork. She glanced at the monitor, at the flashing light and her heart ached. "Danny again."

Samantha pushed aside the papers and hurried down the hall. When she entered the room Danny was shaking his head, pushing away his mother's hand. His poor mom. She tried to comfort him, rubbing her hand up and down his arm, telling him it would be better.

Danny moved away from her, his face tightening in pain. "No."

"Danny, it's okay." Samantha glanced at the monitor, at the vitals that continuously flashed. A monitor his mother probably never stopped watching, no matter how often they told her to ignore it and focus on her son. That monitor meant life. It meant a blood pressure that was either too high or too low, it meant a heart still beating. It meant breaths still being taken. And every beep, every pause, caused a parent's heart to stop.

"It hurts," Danny cried, his hand rubbing his leg.

"I know, sweetie, I know. I'm going to up your pain

meds and we're going to turn down the lights a little. Let your mom hold your hand. Let her pray."

He reached for Samantha's hand and squeezed. "Stay?"

"I'll stay."

She closed her eyes as Danny's mom prayed. For wisdom, for the right treatment to help her son, for strength for her family. For the staff. Samantha felt Danny's fingers relax in her hold. She opened her eyes and looked down at him. He had closed his eyes and though his jaw was still clenched he seemed calmer.

"I'm okay," he whispered. The pain meds were already at work. His mom's prayer had calmed him.

"Of course you are," she assured him, and managed a smile. "You're going to be fine."

He nodded and glanced at his mom, who looked away but not before Sam saw the tears pool in her eyes and break free. She kept Danny busy, talking in low voices until his mom regained her composure.

"I could call someone," Sam offered, taking herself by surprise. "A minister. Danny, would you mind if Remington Jenkins stopped by tomorrow if he isn't busy?"

"Would he?"

"I think he would." She looked to Danny's mom.

"That would be nice," his mom said.

Samantha left his room, waiting until she was in the hall to brush away her tears. As she stood there taking deep breaths and getting hold of herself, a hand touched her back.

The other RN on duty, Annie Jeffers, glanced her way. "You okay?"

Samantha shook her head as she pinched the bridge of her nose. "No, not really. But I will be."

"That's what we keep telling ourselves. It'll get better. Or we'll get used to the pain. Why don't you clock out and head home? I can handle things until the next shift gets here."

"I shouldn't."

"Go. I'm the charge nurse and I'm telling you to go home and get some sleep."

"I won't sleep," Samantha admitted.

Annie Jeffers, tall and thin, brown hair shot through with gray, smiled knowingly. "No, probably not. But you can unwind. See you in a few days, Martin."

"Thank you."

Fifteen minutes later Sam pulled up to her little house. For a few minutes she sat in her truck, enjoying the quiet, the darkness. A full moon illuminated the field and the lawn. The house and barn were dark. She could see her horse moving slowly through the field, grazing, then lifting his head to look around.

She should go riding. It had been years since she'd gone riding this late at night. A full moon and clear skies were almost an invitation to take a midnight ride. But she didn't want to go alone. And Brody, her favorite companion for a midnight ride, was at home with his wife.

She grabbed her phone and scrolled through numbers, stopping at a familiar name.

It seemed like a bad idea even as she dialed.

It seemed like a worse idea when he answered.

"Sam, is everything okay?" His voice was husky, half-asleep.

"I'm sorry. I didn't think you'd be asleep."

"No. It's okay. What do you need?"

She pulled the keys out of her truck and got out. "You won't believe me if I tell you."

"Try me." She pictured him smiling as he said it.

"I want to go riding."

There was a long pause and she imagined him rubbing his hand over his face, trying to wake up. "Riding?"

"Yes, riding. It's a full moon and a clear night. It's like daylight out here."

"Bad night?" he asked with more intuition than she would have liked.

"Just the usual," she replied. Riding was one thing; turning to him was something else altogether.

"I'll be over in a few. Do you have a horse I can ride?"

She didn't. "We can ride double on Buzz."

Another long pause. "I'll bring a horse."

He showed up fifteen minutes later with a truck and trailer. Sam had already saddled Buzz. The poor horse looked confused, but he was a good sport, standing tied to the fence, occasionally trying to reach for a blade of grass that he couldn't quite get to.

Remington backed his horse out of the trailer already saddled. Sam's attention flicked from the dark bay to Remington. He hadn't shaved and the shadow of dark stubble gave him a rugged appeal. His gray eyes were still sleepy. He looked young. And sweet. In his faded jeans and dark blue T-shirt he looked as if he might have just stepped out of her dreams.

"Ready to go?" he asked as he closed up the trailer and led his horse around to face her.

"Yes," she answered.

"Sam, it's really okay to need a friend."

She swung into the saddle and Buzz sidestepped. She handled him, holding the reins steady, and then she glanced back at her riding companion. "I know that, Rem."

"I'm not sure if you do."

"I have friends," she insisted.

"I know."

She settled into the saddle and reined Buzz toward the open gate. "Close that behind you."

"Will do."

The field before them looked like ribbons of silver in the bright light of the moon and with a breeze blowing the grass. Remington brought his horse up next to Buzz.

"You were right—it's a perfect night for this." Remington eased his horse a little closer. "I wasn't sure when you first woke me up. Sleep felt pretty good."

"Sorry about that."

"It's okay. I wouldn't have wanted to miss this."

"I haven't done this in years. Not since... not since the last time we went."

"No?"

She shook her head. "No."

Remington reached for her hand. "Stop."

She looked up, met his gray eyes. He'd left his hat behind and his hair curled ever so slightly.

"Stop what?" she asked.

"Stop thinking so much. You're worrying yourself to death. You wanted this ride to relax, to clear your head, right?" He waited for her to nod. "Then stop thinking and enjoy the ride. We may never have this night again, so enjoy it."

He was right. In a few hours it would be morning and this night would be gone forever.

"We should have brought fishing poles."

He grinned, white teeth flashing against dark skin. "What a good idea. It's always fun to fish in a creek with no fish."

"We used to," she reminded him.

"Yeah, we did." He reached for her hand and she let him take it.

For a long time they rode in companionable silence, their hands clasped, their horses walking almost shoulder to shoulder.

"What happened tonight?" he asked as they circled their horses back around, toward her place.

"Do you think you'd be able to stop by and visit with Danny and his mom? Tomorrow. Or as soon as you can. They would both appreciate it."

"Yes, I can stop by," he said quietly, his hand squeezing hers.

She nearly melted with emotion but couldn't let go. She didn't want to start sobbing. She didn't want to let go and drown in grief. She had taken this job knowing what it meant and what she would have to learn to handle. But there were things a person couldn't prepare for, things one never learned to deal with.

"Thank you," she whispered as his hand continued to hold on to hers.

"Do you want to talk about it?"

"No, I'm good." She released his hand and let her horse break into an easy lope. With the wind in her hair and the horses' hooves eating up the ground, she felt a little freer, a little less tied up in knots.

"Why do you think you have to get through it alone?" Remington asked as they slowed their horses to a walk.

"It's less messy this way, wouldn't you agree?" Because if she didn't rely on people, they didn't let her down. "Rem, I'm good."

Buzz stopped when Remington's horse came to a halt.

"If by good, you mean good at shutting people out, I agree."

"I don't mean to," she said. "It's a habit."

"Break the habit. They say if you do something new for twenty-one days, it becomes a new habit."

She laughed at that. "I think that's a bogus theory."

"Why not give it a try. Twenty-one days of letting me into your life."

"Oh, so the habit I'm supposed to form is you?"

He grinned and she almost gave in. "Would I be such a bad habit?"

"Yes. It took me years to break the Remington habit the last time around."

"This is our present, not our past. Why not see who we are now?"

He moved his horse a little closer and her senses filled up with his presence, his clean soap scent, his smile. How could she see the sweet tilt of his mouth and his carefree wink and not capitulate just a tiny bit?

"Twenty-one days of trusting me. Sharing with me. Getting to know me." He eased a little closer.

"But what happens at the end of the twenty-one days?" She didn't want to find herself ten times lonelier because he would be gone again.

"You'll realize that you're no longer alone. You will

realize you have family to call on and that you have friends in this town. You'll realize you have me."

"Having you is the part that scares me, Rem. Not being who you want me to be scares me," she whispered as he leaned in close and brushed his lips against hers. The kiss stopped her words and she froze, afraid to breathe, afraid she'd wake up and he'd be gone.

She was afraid to hope. And yet she wanted to hope. So very much.

Remington kept his word and stopped by Danny's room the next morning before checking in on Gus. The boy and his mom were sitting together on the edge of his bed, crutches nearby. They greeted him, but he could see that Danny's mom had dark circles under her eyes and looked as if she'd probably cry at the drop of a hat.

"Danny, my friend, you're looking good."

"Thanks, Pastor," Danny pointed at his leg, amputated below the knee. "It's been pretty sore."

"I'm sorry to hear that. Have you been using the prosthesis at all?"

Danny shook his head. "No. And now they think there's more cancer."

Danny's mom choked back a sob. Danny reached for her hand, only ten years old but going on fifty.

"I'm sorry to hear that." He pulled up a chair and sat across from them. "I'd like to pray with the two of you. But I'd also like to bring a friend to visit. His name is Duncan. He's a world-class cowboy and you might have something in common."

Danny grinned at that. "I'd like that."

"Good, I'll give him a call today and see when he can visit. And I want you to do something for me. I want you to remember that God is more than able to get you through this. And when you're troubled, remember that if you ask for peace, He'll give you more peace than you can imagine."

The words seemed simple, too simple. But Remington believed them, and more than anything, he wanted Danny and his mom to find that peace to help them through this situation. He prayed with them, and when he left he thought they looked a little more optimistic.

When he got to Gus's room he found his grand-dad showered, shaved and wearing his own clothes. He looked up from the bag he was packing and gave Remington a hard stare.

"Good grief, son, you look like something a dog wouldn't even bother dragging home." Gus made a face to reflect the words.

"Gee, thanks, Gus."

"Are you sick?" Gus eyed him a little more closely. "You haven't taken to hard drink, have you? That stuff will rot your liver."

"I don't drink." Remington sat down in the chair next to the bed. "I was up late last night."

"Did you have a date?"

He smiled at the memory. "Not exactly."

"Did you see that little Sammy Martin? She's a pretty thing. You know she came down to visit me yesterday evening. She looked about wrung out. She must have had a hard time at work."

The words flew out before he could stop them. "She did." Gus's eyes narrowed.

"Well now, that's something, isn't it?"

"It's nothing, Gus. We're just friends."

"Right, and my left foot isn't bigger than my right."

"Everyone has one foot bigger than the other."

"Well, it's still a true statement."

Remington didn't even try to make sense of that. "Are you about ready to head home?"

"That's a silly thing to ask a man who's been locked up for a couple of days."

"You aren't in jail," Remington reminded.

"It sure feels like jail. I don't see you volunteering for time in this place."

"I'm not sick."

"Of course you're not." Remington smiled at the woman standing there, looking as if she hadn't been up all night, too.

Samantha stepped into the room, her blond hair pulled back, pink gloss on her lips and blue scrubs with a cartoon character he probably would have recognized if he had kids.

"Well, there's our girl." Gus looked a little too pleased for Remington's peace of mind.

Samantha must have noticed because she halted and looked back toward the door as if she was thinking of bailing. "I have to be at work but I wanted to check on you first. It looks as if you're in good hands, though."

"I'll take you over him any day of the week." Gus motioned her toward the other chair.

Remington had never been sorrier than he was at that moment. "Gus…"

"Rem, I'm just glad to see Sam. She even brought me some magazines to read the other day. The kind with 'Elvis was an alien' stories. I love those."

"I'm sure you do." Remington would give anything to be abducted by aliens at that exact moment.

"I've been wondering," Gus started. "Why don't the two of you just make up and get married."

A quick look at Sam proved she was beyond speechless, her mouth actually hanging open. She obviously didn't know his granddad as well as she thought. They said the TIAs and the stroke had taken away his filter. Remington didn't agree. Gus had always been this way, now he just guarded it a little less carefully.

"Gus, I don't think we should be having this conversation," Remington warned, but he knew Gus wouldn't listen. His granddad should wear a sign warning people that he thought his age gave him the right to say whatever he wanted.

"I'm not sure why we should avoid the elephant in the room," Gus quipped with a grin that waggled his mustache. "I'd sure like to have some great-grandchildren before I pass on to my eternal reward."

"I'm not sure it's going to be that rewarding, Gus."

Samantha laughed and got up from the chair. "Well, I'm afraid I'm going to have to leave the two of you to sort this all out. Gus, take care and make sure you drive them all a little bit crazy."

He winked at her. "You got it, Sam. And you try to have a better day."

Remington watched her leave, then turned his attention back on his grandfather.

"You pull a stunt like that again and I'll leave you here to find your own way home."

With a gnarled hand Gus waved off the threat. "Son, you don't have what it takes to catch that little gal on your own."

"Why do you think that?"

"Parker told me you don't have game." Gus eased out

of the bed and sat in the chair Samantha had left empty. "I'm not sure what that means exactly but I think it has something to do with the fact that she's here and you're here, but you haven't done much more than aggravate her. Although she did seem a mite happier to see you this morning."

"We went riding last night. End of story. And I don't think I'm going to take dating advice from a nine-year-old and an eighty-year-old."

"I'm seventy-nine. And you need to take my advice. That little gal is something special."

"I know that."

"Then ask her out."

He leaned toward his grandfather. "Gus, we have a history that doesn't bear repeating. She's a little gun-shy and I'm not going to rush into something."

Gus tugged on his mustache and underneath it a grin lurked. "Well, I guess you're smarter than I thought."

"Isn't that why I'm here?"

Gus chuckled. "Well, you've always been my favorite. Guess that's not a secret."

"You're my favorite, too. And you'd best take care of yourself because I'm not ready to run that ranch alone."

"I won't have a choice. That sister of mine told me she's tossed out all the frying grease and my snack cakes. She said I'd best get used to baked food and low-fat everything."

"Good for her."

Gus didn't agree, but his argument was cut off by the nurse entering the room. She was a little older than Remington, but Gus didn't seem to mind. He flirted, winked and had her turning three shades of red as she helped him gather up his belongings and explained the doctor's orders.

After Gus had been officially released by the doctor, they headed back to Martin's Crossing. As they drove through town, Gus pointed to Main Street.

"Can we stop at Duke's for coffee? And I wouldn't mind buying a few things at the store."

The grocery store was directly across from Duke's No Bar and Grill. But Remington was a little suspicious on that front. "What do you want from the store?"

"I'm a grown man with an addiction to cream-filled chocolate cakes."

Remington laughed at his confession. "Well, I'm not going against Aunt Lee. You take that up with her. But I will take you to Duke's for coffee."

The diner had quite a lunch crowd that day, forcing Remington and Gus to take a seat with Boone Wilder, Duke Martin and a few others.

"Rem, I'd heard you were back in town," Boone said as he poured sugar in his coffee. Remington had heard from locals that after a stint in the army and time spent in Afghanistan, Boone and a couple of friends had started a bodyguard-and-security business.

"Yeah, I'm helping Gus at the ranch."

"You going to be riding this weekend?"

Remington knew he meant the local rodeo. It was a bimonthly event in Martin's Crossing from May through October. This year he'd heard they planned on culminating with a fair and a bigger-than-usual championship event.

"I think so. I've got a nice gelding that shows promise in calf roping."

Boone nodded and took a sip of coffee that had to be syrup by now, he'd put so much sugar in it.

Ned, the waitress who kept the place going, appeared with a pot of coffee. "Gus, it's good to see you back home. Coffee?"

"Coffee and a piece of chocolate pie." Gus winked at her as he ordered.

"Gus!" Remington only halfheartedly protested. If a man got to be Gus's age by eating snack cakes and fried food, what would an occasional piece of chocolate pie hurt him?

"I'm having my pie."

"I know you are." Remington smiled at Ned. "And I'll take one, too."

Ned filled both their cups with coffee. As she walked away, Remington returned his attention to the men at the table. Brody Martin wouldn't look at him. Duke glared. He had a bad feeling about that. The last thing he wanted was to tangle with the Martins. But if he had to, he would. Because this time he wasn't letting them run him off. He had as much right to be here as they did.

And he wasn't going to walk away from Samantha.

Chapter Eleven

By the time Friday rolled around, Samantha was ready for a day off. She needed groceries, she needed to eat lunch with someone other than herself and she needed fresh air. The day was hers to do with as she pleased. Until evening. She'd promised Lilly they would work their horses in the evening, after the sun went down and it cooled off a bit.

She pulled her truck into an empty parking space in front of the grocery store. Last year it had been bought by a family from Dallas who wanted small-town life. It was now known as Gaston's Market. She was glad the store had remained in business. It was such a part of Martin's Crossing, that wood-sided building with century-old architecture, big windows in the front. The inside was small, just a few aisles and it still had the original hardwood floors. The store also had a meat counter with fresh meat each day.

Before she made it inside, Oregon stepped out the front door of Oregon's All Things. The little store, along with Lefty's, were just to the left of the grocery store.

"Sam, I haven't seen you in ages." Oregon let the door

of her shop close behind her. Her dark hair was pulled back and she wore an apron over a paisley skirt and peasant blouse. Her hands were splattered with paint.

"It has been a while." Sam drove past Oregon and Duke's house every day. She saw Lilly almost daily. But Oregon was usually busy with the shop or kid stuff.

"We should have lunch. Are you off today?" Oregon said, pausing as a big truck, too loud to hear over, went down the road.

"Yes, I'd love to have lunch."

It was time for her to become better acquainted with these new sisters of hers. She'd been home a couple of months, and in that time she'd been busy. Too busy to connect with family.

Oregon's eyes widened. "Really? You'll have lunch with me?"

"Did you suggest it because you thought I'd say no?"

Oregon laughed. "No, of course not. I just didn't expect a yes."

"On my way to town I was thinking it would be nice to hang out with someone."

"Someone other than my daughter?" Oregon teased.

"Never. I love that girl."

"She feels the same way. It's been said that the two of you are a lot alike. I was starting to doubt that. You've been so quiet since you've come home."

There were underlying questions within that statement, which she dodged. "I need to get groceries, then I'll be ready for lunch."

"If you have anything to keep cold, you can put it in the fridge in back of my shop. Did you know that Kayla is going to be in town?"

"The missing sister is going to make her presence known again? Did she say where she's been?"

"No, just that if she'd wanted to be found, she would have let everyone know."

Samantha shook her head. Kayla, their half sister, was two years her junior and twice as wild. She had a chip on her shoulder and too much money at her disposal. They didn't know each other that well but Samantha and her brothers worried anyway. Like them, Kayla Stanford had been abandoned by their mother. Her father, a lawyer and aspiring politician, had little to do with his daughter, other than to keep her bank account full. Kayla, as wild as she seemed, did care for the mother who had left them all behind.

"Okay, get your shopping taken care of and when you're ready, we'll go to lunch. I have it on good authority that my husband has homemade French bread for lunch."

"That sounds perfect."

Once her shopping was finished, Samantha hurried back to Oregon's, going in through the back door. After storing her groceries in the fridge, Samantha found her sister-in-law in the front of the store with customers who said they'd stopped in Martin's Crossing while on their way to San Antonio. Samantha browsed while they talked. She stopped at a rack of pretty dresses in spring colors.

By the time the customers finished paying and walked out the door, Samantha had her arms full of her own purchases. She walked up to the register and dropped the clothing on the counter.

"I've been shopping," Samantha said. "If you'd put these behind the counter, I'll pay when we get back from lunch."

Oregon hung the dresses, skirts and tops on a bar hanging from the wall. "Sure thing. Let's go to lunch."

They walked across the street and up the steps to Duke's.

"Inside or out?" Samantha asked when they reached the long porch with tables and chairs for outside dining. Ceiling fans mounted on the overhang turned slowly, creating a breeze.

"With the weather this beautiful, definitely out," Oregon said. "Pick a table and I'll tell Duke we're here."

"No offense, but tell him he can't join us."

Oregon gave her a curious look. "Will do."

When Oregon returned, Samantha had found a table at the far end of the deck. Ned followed Oregon out the door. The waitress carried a tray with water glasses, the coffeepot and flatware.

"Do you gals want coffee?" Ned raised the pot in the air after setting water glasses in front of them. "As warm as it is, I can't imagine drinking the stuff. But who am I to judge?"

"No coffee. I'll take water and I'd like a chef salad and a slice of Duke's French bread," Sam said, glancing at Oregon.

"The same for me." Oregon said.

"Okeydokey, salads and French bread it is." Ned wrote it down and hurried off, faster than any woman her size should move. She was a dynamo. Not only did she work full-time for Duke, but she ran the ranch her parents had left her. She'd been married once, a long time ago. He'd left her and she'd never remarried.

Of course, like most stories there were several different versions when it came to the tale of Nedine and her ex-husband.

After Ned walked away, Oregon sat there for a few minutes, pretending interest in the condensation that dripped down her glass.

"Go ahead, ask." Samantha tapped a fork on the table to get Oregon's attention.

"Ask what?" Oregon glanced up, making quick eye contact before a hint of a smile touched her lips.

"You have questions you want to ask me?"

"Oh. Yes. Questions." Oregon leaned forward. "Duke was up late the other night. He saw Remington's truck leaving your place."

Ned returned with salads and a basket of warm French bread.

"Here you go, ladies. Anything else?"

"No thanks, Ned. This looks wonderful." Sam grabbed a piece of the bread. She slathered it with butter and took a bite, closing her eyes to savor the taste. "My brother is a culinary genius."

"He is," Oregon agreed. "Duke is a culinary genius, and an overprotective, overimaginative brother. He made wild assumptions about Remington's truck at your place."

"He can unruffle those Martin feathers because Remington and I are just friends."

"That's usually the best place to start."

"It isn't a start of anything." Or at least that was what she kept telling herself. She didn't know anymore. "We went riding. There was a full moon."

"I see."

She chased away the thoughts and met Oregon's cautious gaze. "Honestly, I don't know what it is between us, Oregon. I just know that I don't want to get hurt again. I can't lose another piece of myself."

"A relationship doesn't require you to give up anything."

"Doesn't it?" she asked. "I think it might. I'm very good at losing people."

Oregon's hand reached for hers, giving it a light squeeze. "Oh, honey, I'm so sorry. Your brothers are big, overprotective idiots. They meant to do the right thing."

"I know they did." Suddenly, she felt like she was going to cry. She closed her eyes and breathed deep. "This is why I avoid girl lunches. All of this sharing."

Soft laughter answered that remark. "That's part of the fun, Sam. We share. We complain together and cry together and laugh together. We get other perspectives. My perspective, if you want it…" Oregon paused.

Samantha nodded. "I think I do."

"Give Remington a chance. Give your brothers a chance. Give yourself a chance."

"That's taking a lot of chances." Samantha didn't mind taking risks. She'd been hang gliding. She'd tried skydiving and scuba diving. She'd gone mountain climbing in Colorado. But taking chances with her heart? Since Remington, she'd kept dating light and easy, nothing serious, nothing that involved getting hurt.

"Speaking of chances. This might be yours." Oregon inclined her head toward the street. "There's Remington."

Samantha didn't turn around immediately. She was proud of herself for that little bit of control. A few minutes later Remington came up the ramp, pushing Parker in front of him. The boy waved happily and Remington nodded once.

"Sam, we're going to the park," Parker announced.

"To the park?" she looked from the boy to Remington.

"We have a basketball and we're going to shoot

hoops," Remington answered, casual, as if it wasn't a big deal. She noticed then that he was wearing shorts and tennis shoes. She also noticed that he had really nice legs.

She cleared her throat. "That sounds great."

"Will you come with us?" Parker grabbed the wheels of the chair and headed her way without Remington. The man looked a little flummoxed. Samantha liked that look on him. It made him more human.

Why not join them for basketball?

"I'd love to. I have to take my groceries home but by the time I get back the two of you should be finished with your lunch."

"Awesome," Parker raised a hand for a fist bump and she obliged as she looked over his head at Remington.

"Day one," Remington said.

Sam narrowed her eyes, unsure. Then it dawned on her. His twenty-one-day challenge. He thought this was step one in making him a habit.

"It's a game of basketball, Rem."

"Yes, just a game of basketball," he agreed. "See you in a little while."

After he and Parker went inside Duke's, Oregon cleared her throat. "Day one?"

"Oh, it's nothing, just a challenge. I hadn't planned on taking it, but I might," she answered her sister-in-law but her mind drifted to what it would take to make Remington a habit she couldn't let go of.

She worried it might take less than twenty-one days. Which meant she needed to guard her heart a little more carefully.

Day one. Remington watched as Samantha made her way down the sidewalk past the Martin's Crossing

Community Church toward the town park. It wasn't much of a park. Just a large lawn and a few flowers. There was a swing set, a teeter-totter and a merry-go-round. But there was also a small basketball court. On one end was a basketball net at standard height. The other end had a lowered net for children.

Parker was at what would have been about the free-throw line, taking aim at that basket. He missed, but not by much. The ball hit the backboard and bounced back. He turned and went after it. Out of the corner of his eye, Remington watched as Sam approached, cautiously, as if she might change her mind at the last second.

He wasn't going to let her change her mind.

"Hey, Parker, look who joined us. I say we play a game. Me against the two of you." Remington shot her a knowing smile.

She narrowed her eyes at him but returned the gesture in a way that appeared more like a challenge. "That sounds like a good plan to me. Parker, what do you think?"

"We'll beat you," Parker boasted. He had the ball and he passed it to Samantha. "Girls first."

She caught the ball, spun and took off. Remington went after her, faking to the right and then circling to try to take the ball. She passed to Parker and the kid did a worthy job of dribbling from the side of his chair. The ball hit the wheel and rolled. Samantha grabbed it and gave it a gentle pass to the boy. Parker went in for another shot. This time he made the basket.

Remington cheered and Sam gave the kid a high five, mussing his hair the way he hated. "That's two-zip," Parker announced with a big grin. "You're going down, loser."

Remington laughed. "Not so fast. I've got moves you haven't seen."

Samantha went after the ball, stealing it from him when her nearness made him lose focus for a moment. She smelled good. He wanted to lean in and breathe deep of the outdoors and the fresh scent she wore.

She held the ball as he moved in close to steal it.

She tossed the ball to Parker and gave Remington a light push to get him out of her space but her hands lingered on his shoulders. When their eyes met, he wondered if she felt it the way he did, that connection, as if everything in the past had brought them to this place, together. But no, she didn't. She was fighting too hard to not feel it. But as her hands moved away he saw a flash in her blue eyes, something that indicated she did feel something for him, and denying it wouldn't make it go away.

"Hey, that's a foul." Parker wheeled around next to them, nine years old and totally unaware.

"Yes, a foul. On your team." Remington grinned at the woman just a head shorter than his six feet. She backed away from him, taking a sharp breath and putting distance between them.

"Totally foul," she agreed.

Parker tossed Remington the ball. "Free throw line."

Remington doubted they were playing basketball by the real rules, but he took the ball and made the shot. Sam grabbed the ball and tossed it to Parker.

"Will you come back to church Sunday?" Remington asked Sam as she moved in place to block him.

She looked surprised by the question. "I hadn't planned on it. I work Sunday nights and…" She shrugged.

"You're not ready?"

"No, I'm not ready. Not for church, or for this." She stepped away from Parker. "It's not easy, Rem. I definitely can't walk into church being the person you want me to be."

He took a quick glance at Parker. The kid had taken himself off to throw practice shots. "And what is it I expect of you?"

"You're the preacher. You have a role to fill. You need a woman who can stand next to you and fit."

He stepped close. "You fit perfectly."

"Not what I meant."

He slid his arms around her waist and pulled her close, mindful that Parker was watching. "See how perfectly you fit?"

She pushed him back, laughing. "Stop."

He bent close to her lips. "I could go on."

"Gross." Parker made a gagging noise like a typical nine-year-old, which meant he'd lost interest in practicing.

"Not too gross, my friend." Remington leaned in and gave her a chaste kiss. He had to back away or he wouldn't be able to think.

"Not gross," Samantha conceded. "But I meant it, Rem. I don't play the piano. I can't bake a casserole."

"What are you talking about?"

"You need a woman who can do those things. I think it's in the handbook somewhere about pastor's wives."

"You're going to be my wife?" He smiled. "This twenty-one-day challenge is working out better than I expected."

She rolled her eyes and huffed her outrage, which didn't sound as outraged as she'd intended. "No, I'm not going to be your wife. I'm telling you that you're barking up the wrong tree."

"Because I'm so perfect, I walk on water?"

"Rem, stop. We both know what I mean."

"Yeah, I guess." He studied her face, the flush of her cheeks bringing out the blue in her eyes. "But your faith isn't completely gone."

"No, it isn't. I'm realizing it isn't my faith I lost. At least not my faith in God. More like I lost faith in people."

"That's understandable. But there are a lot of people in this world and not all of them believe sitting in a church pew is the same as sitting in a courtroom on the jury."

Parker had left them alone again. Remington watched the boy trying to make a shot on the higher net. He admired that he had no quit in him. Remington guessed he was taking a page from Parker's book. He wasn't going to quit.

"Come to church. Twenty-one days, remember?"

Samantha glanced away from him. A few strands of blond hair had come loose and the breeze whipped them across her cheek.

"Sam?" he spoke softly, gaining her attention.

"Maybe." She gave him a careful look, blue eyes veiled, hiding whatever she felt. "I should go."

"Stay a little longer. I promise to give you a break."

"Really? What if I tell you, you get no breaks from our team?" She jogged to Parker's side. The boy tossed her the basketball and she dunked it before giving it back to him.

Parker wheeled himself to the other end of the court, back to Remington's side. The game was on. The boy had a determined set to his mouth and his eyes narrowed in on the basket.

Remington moved in to take the ball but Parker caught it up and put distance between them. Life wasn't perfect. It had its challenges, but this was victory. Parker smiling, having a good time, made everything worthwhile.

They made a good team. He and Parker. And Samantha.

That thought felt a little dangerous when he considered her declaration that she couldn't be who he needed her to be. He wanted Sam, the person she used to be. He didn't know if she still existed or if life had buried her beneath the rubble of heartache and loss.

But he was willing to find out.

Chapter Twelve

Dust kicked up from the arena as the second participant in the junior event rounded the barrels Saturday evening. Samantha stood outside the fence and watched the girl lean over the neck of her horse, urging the big paint toward the exit and the finish line. She held tight to the fence, yelling when the girl yelled. It couldn't be helped. She loved this sport. The exhilaration of it made her heart pound and her breath catch. Fifteen to twenty seconds of sheer adrenaline rush.

After that ride she went looking for Lilly. She walked behind the stands, saying hello to neighbors and to people she no longer knew. She'd been gone so long. Everyone had changed. She'd changed most of all.

Almost to the trailers, she heard someone call her name. She looked around and saw Jake's wife, Breezy, as she hurried to catch up. The twins weren't with her, but baby Irene was strapped to her front in a little pink pouch. The sight brought a lurch to her heart.

It reminded her of what she'd lost.

But the loss was getting easier to deal with. It had been getting easier for a while now; she just hadn't realized it until lately. The ache, the empty space in her heart where her daughter should have been, would always be there. But she thought it was filling up a little.

She'd done something for a family that they couldn't do for themselves. She'd answered their prayers for a child. It was hard to comprehend it, that her pain turned into their blessing. But she was trying.

She was finding herself again. After years of avoiding her home, her brothers and her faith, she was finding her way back.

"Hi, Breezy," she greeted her sister-in-law. Tall, elegant Breezy with her open smile and easy laugh. When Samantha tried to play the victim card, she thought of her sister-in-law abducted away from her siblings and living homeless for much of her life.

"Hey, Jake said to find you and see if you want your horse saddled."

Her brothers, always trying to take care of everything. "I'm heading that way now. But first I wanted to check on Lilly. I would miss my own ride before I'd miss hers. She's so excited."

"She's overwhelmed," Breezy acknowledged as she leaned to kiss Irene's dark, curly hair. "She has you here. That's everything to her. Oregon said she's talked nonstop all day."

Samantha could picture that. "She's something else. I'm blessed by all of these pretty nieces. And now a nephew or two to add to the package."

Breezy gave her a careful look but kept quiet. The two of them walked together to the Circle M trailer. Jake had recently bought the four-horse trailer with living quarters. Duke had brought a second trailer for his horse and Lilly's.

Her brother Brody was busy working over the hooves of one horse, cleaning out a stone that had gotten lodged. He had the horse's hoof raised, a pick poised when the animal moved, bumping against him. He tightened his grip on the foreleg and held it firmly as he leaned into the horse's shoulder.

"Hold on," he growled.

"Want help?" Samantha offered as she walked up, reaching for the horse's bridle.

"I've got him. He's Duke's new animal and he doesn't have any manners."

"You should tell him you're ten years away from knee replacement and he might be more respectful."

"Ha, ha, funny." He picked out a small stone and let the horse's leg down.

"I try." Samantha ran a hand down the horse's face. "He's got mean eyes."

"He's okay." Brody patted the gelding's neck. "Where's your horse?"

"In the trailer. I'm going to get him out in a minute. Where's your wife?"

"Grace is at home with a sick baby." He stepped away from the trailer he'd been leaning against.

"Anything I can do? If she needs a break, I'm here."

"I'll let her know."

"Okay. Well, I'm going to find Lilly and make sure she's doing okay." Samantha started to walk away and Brody walked alongside her. "Is there something else?"

"I wanted to remind you that Grace and I are going to Dallas." To see their mother. He didn't have to tell her that; she knew.

"You've asked before," she reminded.

"I know that. I'm going to keep offering." He shifted,

pushing his hat back, narrowing his deep blue gaze on her. He was closest to her in age. Like her, he had few memories of their mother. The day their mother drove off into the sunset she'd beaten him, leaving him battered and bruised. He'd been little at the time, a preschooler, and he'd blocked the memory for the longest time.

"I'll go when I'm ready."

"Sammy," he started.

Anything he planned to say was cut off when someone walked up behind her. "Give her a break.

"Brody, she said she doesn't want to go." Remington stepped next to Samantha, offering her a good-natured wink as his shoulder bumped hers.

"Stay out of this, Rem." Brody kept walking. His lean jaw was set, unsmiling, and he didn't give. "This is important."

"Yeah, it is. But Sam will go when she's ready."

"I'm a grown woman. I don't need a brother pushing me to do something I don't want to do. I might never want to do it." She turned to Remington. "I don't need you interfering, either."

"I'm just trying to help," he said, tugging his hat down just a smidge so that he looked cute, making it hard for Sam to stay angry with him. "I'm being 'here for you.'"

Brody had the nerve to laugh. "I think my job here is done."

He strolled away, leaving her with Remington. They stood there, facing each other, the rodeo arena behind them, the people in the stands just a vague hum of activity in the distance. It all faded and it was just the two of them.

"I don't need your help with my brother," she repeated.

"I know you don't. But I'm here and I'm going to push my way into your life. I'm going to be here for you." He touched his fingers to hers. "You might as well let me in."

Let him in. Temptation came in the form of a too-handsome-for-words cowboy with scruffy whiskers covering his suntanned cheeks and gray eyes that twinkled with amusement. And something else. The temptation wasn't even the kind that would send her to the altar on Sunday morning. It made her want to give them another chance.

And that frightened her. Because letting him in meant taking the chance she might lose him again.

If she lost anyone else, she wasn't sure she could handle it.

"It's day three," he teased.

"Two," she countered. "You're not a habit yet."

"No, but I'm not giving up. They just called the juniors division. You don't want to miss Lilly."

"No, I don't."

His hand closed around hers and he led her to the arena to watch as another barrel racer crossed the finish line. Lilly was up next. Samantha could see her readying her horse behind the gate. Duke was with her, as he should be. Samantha saw Lilly look her way. She waved to let her know she was there, watching.

Her heart hesitated when the gate opened and Lilly's horse rushed out. The girl leaned, the horse stretched out, his neck long, his stride perfect. They took the first barrel a little wide. Samantha clenched her jaw, holding tight to the rail.

"Take a breath—she's fine." Remington leaned close, his shoulder against hers. When she took a breath she smelled him, the fresh scent of soap, shampoo and leather.

"Of course she's fine," Samantha agreed. And Lilly was fine. She took the second barrel, close but not too close. She rounded the third barrel with ease and hit the home stretch, her horse giving her everything he had.

When she crossed the finish line, the announcer's voice on a sketchy PA system told the crowd that they had a new leader. And since she was the last rider in the junior division, Lilly was the winner.

Samantha let out a whoop as her niece rode back into the arena for her trophy. Strong arms grabbed Samantha up and twirled her around. She looked down into the face of the cowboy who held her tight, lifting her feet off the ground. His gray eyes sparkled and the look he gave made her giddy on the inside.

As he set her feet back on the ground, she stood on tiptoe and kissed his cheek. But then she quickly made excuses about saddling her horse and walked away. Because he was too much. Being near him was too much.

Remington let her walk away, but he wasn't going to let her go for good. Not this time. Ten years ago he'd loved her the way seventeen-year-old boys loved. He hadn't been thoughtful. He hadn't really been respectful. Now that he thought about it, he'd let her down on so many levels, it was a wonder she still talked to him.

He wanted to make up for that. He wanted to be there for her. Not just today. No, he wanted to be there for her every day, whether it was a good day or bad.

With that in mind, he headed back to the trailer

where he'd left his horse. The big paint whickered a greeting. Remington leaned to buckle up his chaps, pulled on his gloves and pushed his hat down a little tighter. When he backed his horse out of the trailer, the big gelding raised his black-and-white painted head and looked around. Splash was a little wild-eyed most of the time. But at a rodeo he was dependable and never had a bad day. As wired as he seemed, he knew how to settle when someone was in the saddle.

"Nice horse, Jenkins."

Remington reached into the trailer for his saddle before he returned Brody Martin's greeting. He eased the saddle pad on his horse's back, and then followed with the saddle.

"Thank you." He glanced over the back of his horse at the man standing behind his trailer.

"If you're not serious about my sister, I'd like for you to stay clear of her."

Brody Martin didn't pull any punches, Remington knew. He reached under Splash for the girth strap and pulled it up. He gave it a tug, tightened it, moved the gelding to get him to release a breath and pulled again before buckling the strap.

"Brody, I've got the best of intentions." He reached for the bridle in the storage area where he'd had the saddle. "I had good intentions that summer, but you all saw fit to send me packing."

"She's my kid sister," Brody warned, his voice low.

"Actually, she isn't a kid. She's a woman. A woman I happen to like a lot."

Brody moved away from the back of the trailer. He walked up to the horse and leaned on its back from the off side.

"I wouldn't do that," Remington warned.

"Do what?"

Splash was already shifting, stomping his back leg.

"He doesn't like it when he thinks someone is going to try and mount from his off side. He's kind of peculiar that way."

Brody patted the horse's neck and took a step back.

"I'm going to marry her, Brody."

"Does she know that?" Brody asked.

"Oh, I think she's got an idea of what I have in mind."

Brody stopped smiling. He walked around the rump of the horse and joined Remington. "I don't want to see her hurt."

"I'm not going to hurt her."

"Jake has always regretted sending her away." Brody spoke quietly as the two faced one another.

"He could have let her come home."

Brody shrugged. "He'll never admit it, but he was scared to death. He was trying to make everything right for everyone. Elizabeth had her own stuff going on. We didn't know what to do with Sam."

So they'd sent her away. Remington got mad all over again. The kind of mad that made him want to hit things. He brushed a hand down his face and shifted his attention to Splash. The horse always fought the bridle. And that fight gave Remington a minute to get it together. He held the bit to the horse's mouth and of course Splash tossed his head. But Remington eased the bit in and slipped the bridle in place.

It was funny how things he'd known for years were suddenly harder to hear. When Brody talked about the past so matter-of-factly, it just made him mad. It made him angry with himself.

"I should have found her."

Brody stepped away from the trailer. "Yeah, you could have. But what would you have done? Rode off into the sunset with her? Two teenagers with nowhere to go. Romantic."

"We wouldn't have been the first young couple doing our best to make things right."

"What's past is past. Let it go, Rem."

Brody was probably right. Remington swung into the saddle. Splash moved to the left but settled as Remington found his seat. Brody took a few steps away.

"That horse is a mammoth." Brody grinned as he said it.

"Over sixteen hands," Remington informed him. "He'd eat your horse for lunch."

"He might. But I'll eat yours if you hurt my little sister."

"Could we stop circling like old barn cats? I'm not here to hurt your sister."

Brody gave him a long look. "I didn't say you were. I just came over to help you saddle that horse and thought I'd make conversation. You don't have to be so testy."

Remington unhooked the rope from his saddle. Brody started backing away, hands in the air and a big grin on his face. "I'm going now."

It would have been easy to rope Brody, but Remington let him go. Just then, his phone rang and the caller ID flashed the name of a church member who had been sick for several weeks.

Brody stopped walking as Remington took the call. As he answered he glanced toward the arena. He spotted Samantha on her horse, warming him up before her event. The horse had a lot of energy and she was holding him tight, keeping him in check.

But the call distracted him. He lost sight of her as he listened to the anxious wife on the other end. She'd just called an ambulance for her husband. Remington assured her he would meet her at the hospital.

He rode back to the truck and dropped to the ground, tying Splash and reaching for the girth strap.

"I thought you were riding?" Brody was back, this time standing behind Remington.

"I've got to head to the hospital in Braswell. Chuck Shaw is having trouble breathing."

"I'd heard he'd been down with pneumonia."

"Yeah. He has COPD on top of that." Remington pulled the girth strap loose. "I told Claire I'd meet her."

"Let me get your horse home for you. Unhook your truck from your trailer and I'll hook it up to mine and pull it back to the Rocking J."

"You sure?"

Brody was already lifting the saddle from Splash. "Of course I'm sure. Head on out of here. Claire gets a little lost without Chuck. Is she driving herself to the hospital?"

"I hadn't thought of that. They don't have any kids living around here. I'll call her back and see if I can pick her up. Brody, I appreciate this."

Brody tipped his hat and went back to dealing with Splash, who was never too happy about strangers handling him. "I don't mind at all, brother."

Remington was unhooking the trailer from his truck when Samantha rode up. "Where are you going?"

"Chuck Shaw is on his way to the hospital. He's

having trouble breathing. I'm going to pick up Claire and take her."

Samantha swung a leg over the back of her horse and dropped to the ground. Remington gave her a quick look. She wore a button-up shirt of pale blue, dark jeans and boots with blue stitching. She leaned against the bed of his truck and her horse pushed in close.

"I'll go with you."

The words took him by surprise. He pushed the tongue of the trailer off the hitch of his truck, then looked up at her, thinking he'd probably have it together if he gave himself a few seconds.

"It'll be a long night."

"Yeah, probably. Good thing I'm used to long nights. And Claire." She shrugged. "I've seen her around town with Chuck. She's a little lost without him."

"Yeah, I know. He's been worried about that. He's not sure what will happen to her if he isn't there to take care of her."

"Since Brody is already putting your horse in the trailer, I'll have him take care of mine."

"You were going to ride tonight."

"I'm a big girl, Rem. If I don't get to ride, if I don't get cotton candy at the fair and if I don't have a pretty doll, I'm okay. I want to go. If you want," she added, unsure.

"I want you to go."

She led her horse away. Remington watched as she talked to Brody, and then handed the reins off to her brother. He ignored the look Brody shot him in warning.

Whatever happened between him and Samantha, this time it would be between the two of them and not between them and her brothers.

Chapter Thirteen

It had been a crazy impulse, to tell Remington she would go with him to the hospital. Sitting together with Claire while Chuck was taken in for tests made them appear to be a couple. But they weren't a couple. He was a pastor, and sitting with him as he talked to Claire, encouraging her to have faith and then praying with her—it unsettled Sam.

She opened her eyes as Remington finished praying. The need to escape hit out of nowhere. It wasn't the prayer. It was the need. She hadn't needed anyone in so long. She was afraid of it.

She was afraid of not being the kind of woman he needed.

"I'm going to walk down to the children's unit and check on a few of my kids."

"You have children?" Claire asked, her eyes narrowing.

"No, I'm a nurse, Claire. I'm going to check on the children here at the hospital."

Claire blinked a few times. "Oh, I see. Tell them I said hello."

"I will, sweetie. And I'll be back soon."

Remington excused himself and followed her from the room.

"Are you okay?" His hand was on her arm.

"Of course I am. Did you know you're still wearing chaps?"

"I didn't think about it until I got in here. A pastor in chaps. Well, I guess it could be worse."

If ever a man could pull off a visit to the hospital all scruffy and unshaved with worn leather chaps, it would have to be Remington. She loved that he smelled of dust, leather and horses.

The need to escape grew, but now for other reasons. Or maybe the same reason on a different level. Her feet weren't cooperating, though.

"You know, you actually look pretty irresistible," she whispered.

She started to move away, to escape, but he caught her. His hand on her waist pulled her close. They stood there for a moment, then she finally managed a shaky laugh and put a safe distance between them.

"If I'm irresistible, then why do you keep pulling away," he countered.

"Because I'm not in the market to start any new bad habits."

"I didn't realize I was a bad habit."

"Hmm," she countered. "The worst. And if I snatch you up, all of these nurses will be heartbroken."

"If you don't snatch me up, I'm going to make a fool of myself chasing after you."

She bit down on her bottom lip, suddenly uncomfortable with the teasing because it had managed to get serious. "Don't."

"Don't what, Sam?"

"Just don't." She ran a hand down his arm, wishing she could explain. But it sounded silly, even to her. She was afraid of falling in love again. For twenty-five years she'd wanted someone in her life. Someone to love her. Someone she could love back. A person who would always be there for her.

She knew her brothers loved her. She knew they would come to her rescue at the drop of a hat. But that didn't ease the loneliness.

Her earliest memories were of being passed from sibling to sibling and sometimes to her father, when he was sober. She remembered crying in her bed because she was sick and no one knew. She remembered wanting to be held, to be someone's little girl. Jake had tried. Elizabeth had tried. But in the end, she'd always felt alone.

Until Remington came into her life that summer. And suddenly she'd had someone to belong to. But he'd only been there for a few short months.

Long enough to make her feel even lonelier when he went away.

There had never been anyone to take his place. No one she'd ever dated had made her feel the same, as if she belonged with someone. So it should be easy to fall back in love, to fall back into a relationship.

It would make sense. *They* would make sense.

But what if she couldn't be the person he needed her to be and he walked away again?

"I'm going to check on my kids," she repeated. She needed to hug them, to know that they felt safe and loved.

She needed space to think.

Remington nodded as if he understood and let her go.

The pediatric wing lay in semidarkness with only a couple of nurses slipping from room to room, checking on patients. Samantha felt reassured being here where everything was familiar. Here she knew what was required of her. She knew what she could give and she knew what to expect.

She shot a questioning look at a nurse who walked out of Danny's room, chart in hand. "How is he?"

The nurse kept walking and Samantha fell in step next to her.

"Dr. Jackson is sending him to Dallas. There's a new treatment that might help, and of course everyone wants that for him."

"Of course we do." Samantha heard a tiny sob coming from a nearby room. "Is that Lizzy?"

Nurse Clark nodded, eyes closed. It got to them all at times, the emotion, the sadness in dealing with these children. "Another home fell through. I told them to stop telling her about homes until they know for sure that a family will take her. People tend to not see the child, they see the scars."

"I know." Samantha headed for Lizzy's room. When she stepped through the door into the darkened room lit only with a night-light, Lizzy turned away.

"Hey, daffodil," Samantha whispered as she approached the bed. "I know you're awake. I heard you crying."

A sniffle and a scarred hand brushed at her cheek before slipping beneath the blanket. "I'm not."

Samantha sat down on the edge of the bed and placed a hand on the slim shoulder of the little girl. "I'm sorry."

Lizzy nodded, her blond head moving on the pillow.

"Do you want me to read to you?" Because how

many times in her life as a child had she longed for a mom to read to her? She couldn't be Lizzy's mom, but she could be there for a child. For a little while.

Again that little head nodded.

Samantha pulled the chain on the light and found a book on the table next to the bed. "Cinderella?"

"Too sad."

"It has a happy ending."

A hand slid out from beneath the blanket and swiped her nose. Samantha found a tissue and slipped it into Lizzy's hand. "Use this."

More sniffling. "In Cinderella everyone dies."

Samantha closed her eyes, her heart breaking at those tender, heartfelt words. She wanted to fall apart, but she needed to show Lizzy how to be strong, how to survive.

"But in the end the princess finds someone to love her and she isn't alone anymore."

"Will someone love me?" Lizzy rolled over to face her.

"Someone already does." Samantha kissed the little girl's forehead. "Me. And so many other people. You are loved. And you're not alone. And I believe that God has the perfect home for you."

She meant the words. It had been a long trip, this journey of faith, of finding her way home. But Samantha believed, and she realized she'd never stopped. She'd just been so wounded it had been hard to accept that God had any idea what was going on in her life.

"Cinderella is okay." Lizzy's small voice drew her back.

Samantha started to read, using her brightest, most cheerful whisper voice. As Lizzy's eyes got droopy, Samantha skipped ahead to the happy stuff, to the ball and the prince and the happy-ever-after. Because that's what everyone wanted, to be loved and to have that fairy-tale ending.

Remington stood outside the door, listening to Samantha comfort the little girl. When she began to read, he moved to the side, leaning against the wall and listening to her quiet, sweet voice read the story. A nurse walked by him, nodded, peeked inside the room and kept going.

The story ended with the prince and princess riding away, then Samantha quietly promising a little girl she would pray for her. He stepped into the doorway, aware that what he felt for the woman inside that room was probably written all over his face.

Samantha slipped quietly from the room. They didn't speak. He could see that her emotions were too close to the surface for conversation. But he slipped his arm around her shoulders and pulled her close to his side in order to give her whatever comfort she would allow.

As they left the brightly painted world of the pediatric wing, she asked, "Chuck?"

"Better. They have him on oxygen and he's resting. They're going to keep Claire here so that she won't be alone and confused. If Chuck doesn't get better soon, they think they might have to put her in a residential home for a month or two. She obviously can't be on her own."

"No, she can't. I think most days she's okay, but she isn't entirely safe on her own."

"I called their son. He's coming in the morning and he'll make the final decisions. He would like for them to move to Dallas but I'm not sure if they will."

"Maybe not," she said softly.

"You're very good with these children," he said as he led her out the glass doors to the parking lot. It was still warm. And humid.

"I couldn't imagine doing any other job."

"Do you think we could put the word out, that Lizzy needs a family?"

She leaned her head against his shoulder as they walked.

That gesture felt a little bit like trust. He would walk across coals for the woman at his side. He'd do the same for any child on that unit because it meant something to her.

"We could do it without giving details," she finally answered. They stopped at his truck. "I'm sorry for walking away from you earlier."

"Why did you?"

Remington reached for the door but didn't open it. He wanted an answer. He wanted to hear her admit whatever it was that caused her to run.

"I needed to see those children to remind myself that I'm blessed. I'm so blessed. I don't want to forget that or get too wrapped up in my own sad little story. Because I'm here. I'm happy. I have a job I love. I have people in my life who love me."

"Yes, you do." He reached for her. As he pulled her close, their gazes locked and he heard the hitch in her breath. He bent to touch his lips to hers but stopped just short of making contact.

Her eyes fluttered and closed, but she didn't turn away. He took that as an invitation and his lips moved over hers, tasting the sweetness of strawberry gloss as he lingered. Her hands moved to his shoulders and then up. He felt her fingers brush against the nape of his neck and then she slid them into his hair. He pulled her a little closer.

She broke the kiss, turning her head away just a fraction. "Rem."

He waited, wondering what it was that she couldn't accept about them.

"This is just too much. I'm not sure if this is us now or us trying to find something we left behind."

"Maybe what this is, Sam, is unfinished business. We left something behind that was meant to be and we're finding it again."

"Picking up where we left off?" She moved her hand from his neck to his cheek. "I'm not sure it works that way. I don't think you can take a summer romance between two kids and make it into something that lasts."

"I'm not sure why that wouldn't work."

She scraped her fingers across the day's growth of whiskers that covered his cheeks. That gesture made him want to kiss her again.

"Rem, just the fact that you can say that is proof that we're two different people. You believe anything can happen. I question why it would."

"What if you step to my side of the fence and try optimism?" He glanced at his watch. "It's Sunday. That means we've made it another day in the twenty-one-day challenge. Seventeen days until I'm a new habit you've formed."

He kissed her again before she could protest. He smiled into her lips and felt her return the gesture before she pulled away.

"That isn't fair," she charged, with a twinkle in her blue eyes.

"Maybe not, but I'm determined to have you for my princess."

"So now you're Prince Charming?"

"Yeah, for this situation, you can call me Prince Charming. I'm here to take you away from your normal life." He laughed. "I can't believe you have me talking in fairy tales. It isn't right. I'm going to break a horse tomorrow. The meanest horse I can find."

"To ensure you still have your man card?"

"Yes. And once I prove that to myself, I'm going to take you to dinner."

"I work tomorrow evening."

"Are you coming to church in the morning?"

She shook her head. "No, I'm not. I don't want people in your church to start thinking we're a couple. They'll expect me to bring casseroles and make visits with you."

"Would it be so bad, us as a couple?"

She glanced away from him, biting her bottom lip as she studied the night sky. "I know who I am, Rem. I'm broken. I'm flawed. I couldn't stand next to you and pretend I'm anything more than a person who has made mistakes."

"We're all broken and flawed, Sam. That's the beauty of it. We don't have to be perfect."

"No, of course not." And she managed to sound as if she truly meant it. But he saw the shadow of doubt flicker through her eyes.

He opened the truck door for her because it was time for him to invoke his constitutional rights. The right to remain silent. Because when he pictured his future, he pictured her next to him.

Even if it meant burned casseroles.

Chapter Fourteen

Samantha ran a hose to the water trough and stared out over the field, still half-asleep from her late night at the hospital with Remington. Buzz wandered up and stuck his nose in the water, swishing gently and then pushing his face directly into the stream of water. He lifted his head and blew, showing his teeth in a big horse grin.

His antics made her smile. "You, sir, are nuts."

She shoved the hose down into the trough and went inside the barn to check on Lady and her puppies. She leaned over the door of the stall and watched as the mamma dog played with her pups, nudging and then running around them so that they barked and tried to chase her.

What in the world was she going to do with a dog and nine puppies?

"We'll have to find your puppies new and very loving homes, Lady. But you I have plans for." The dog moved to push her head against Samantha's outstretched arm. "I think you would make a very fine pet-therapy animal. Your big eyes and long, floppy ears make you especially sweet."

Lady looked up at her with those big, sad eyes and Samantha felt her mouth tug in response. "See, you even make me happier."

When she walked outside to turn off the water, Brody was pulling up. Grace and their baby girl, Bria, were with him. She headed for their truck. When she got there, she leaned in the passenger window to catch a glimpse of her niece in her car seat.

"What are you all up to today?" Samantha asked as she opened the rear passenger door of the extended cab truck.

A glimpse of that baby girl through the window just wasn't enough. Bria had the same effect on a person as Lady. Maybe more. Samantha sat down on the edge of the seat, and made faces that a person only makes when speaking to infants.

"We're on our way to church." Brody turned in his seat. "We thought we'd see if you want to go. We're having dinner at Breezy and Jake's after."

"I was up late. I don't think…"

Brody cut her off. "Sam, we're a family. We've all given you space. But it's time for you to join in. We have dinner as a family on Sundays. We're not kids anymore."

"No, you're not," she agreed.

"Then come and find your place in the family." Brody started the truck. "You might want to close that door."

"What?"

"We're going to church," he said as he shifted into Reverse.

"Brody, not this way," Grace chided, the sweet voice of reason.

"I'm not going to church like this." She pointed to the faded jeans and canvas sneakers she'd worn to the barn.

"If I let you run in and change, you won't go to church at all."

"I think most people believe in free will, Brody."

"I'm not talking about church. Your faith is up to you. I'm tired of playing this game. It's time to take your place in this family. We're all in this together, the four of us."

"Five. Don't forget Kayla."

He laughed. "How could anyone forget Kayla? She was on the news last night. She led the police in Austin on a low-speed chase."

"She's just trying to rile her dad," Samantha defended.

"Right. But today isn't about Kayla Stanford. Today is about the Martins, and you."

"I have to work this afternoon," she said, then leaned in to blow on Bria's sweet cheeks. The baby giggled. Samantha glanced up and smiled at Brody. "I'll go to church. I'm not going to miss out on any more of my family. There are all of these sweet babies and I want to be the best aunt ever."

"Close the door, then."

"I'll drive myself. Rem invited me to Countryside." She got out of the truck and closed the door carefully, and then moved over to speak to her brother and his wife. "Grace, I don't know how you put up with him."

"I don't know what I'd do without him," Grace answered.

"Blech." Samantha made a face. "I'll see you all later."

Brody didn't put the truck in Reverse. "We'll just join you at Countryside."

"Fine, I'll meet you there."

And she kept her word. She walked through the doors of the little country church as the pianist began to pound out a song that sounded something like "The Old Rugged Cross." People were singing loud and a few were clapping. Her gaze drifted from the piano to the stage to Remington. As she found a seat on a back pew, she asked herself what it would be like, to allow herself to love him and to be loved by him. When the congregation changed to a new song she tried to join in but her heart got tripped up, wondering if she could survive losing him again.

It was a silly thought, because she knew it was already too late. She was already knee-deep in this situation, already falling. Or maybe her heart had taken up where it left off ten summers ago. Whatever the case, she already knew he could hurt her. She'd known it all along.

The music ended. Remington stood, clipping a mic to his collar, smiling at the congregation. She pushed aside all of the other thoughts swirling around in her head to focus on his words. As he talked about faith, about doubts, she realized he belonged in this place, in this church.

She could see it in his words, in his expression and in the way the people filling the pews listened. If a man truly had a calling, it was this one.

After the service ended, she found Brody and Grace, Bria asleep in her daddy's arms. They stood up and were gathering their belongings when she approached.

"You could have sat with us," Brody said as he slung

the strap of the pink backpack over his shoulder. She smiled a little and he quirked one brow. "What?"

"Nothing. Pink looks good on you."

Brody shook his head. "Thanks. I bought it because it matches my eyes."

"Sam." Remington appeared at her side. "I thought I might introduce you to a few people."

She shook her head. "I have to go. I'm expected at lunch. But thank you."

"Chicken?" he teased as he stepped close, letting people walk past.

"Not at all."

He opened his mouth to say more, no doubt to tease, but an older gentleman approached, tapping him on the shoulder. "Pastor, we were wondering if we could have a quick meeting with you."

"Of course, Jerry. Anything in particular?" Remington glanced at his watch. "How long will it take so I can let Gus and Lee know?"

"It shouldn't take that long. We just wanted to have a last-minute discussion on the help we're giving to the family that lost their home to fire."

"I'll be right there." And then he refocused on Sam. "Sixteen days to go, Sam."

She had started to walk away, but she stopped. "Rem, take care of your church and your family."

"I'm a great multitasker," he assured her as he walked away.

Outside the sun was bright and warm. People were talking in small groups. A few of them she knew and she waved or nodded a greeting. She ignored the ones who studied her as if she were a bug under a microscope. She bristled under their scrutiny and knew that later she would be topic number one at lunch. "Wasn't she the one…" is how the conversations would begin.

She told herself it didn't matter. What mattered more was who she had become. She wondered why people never thought about that. Why didn't they think about her reasons for doing the things she'd done? Why hadn't any of them stepped in to help her, to guide her, to figure out what was wrong? Instead, they'd waited until her proverbial train went off the tracks, and then they'd all had something to say.

Grace gave her a cautious look. "Are you okay?"

"Of course I am," Sam said.

"For a minute there, you looked like a storm cloud bearing down on us."

She smiled at her sister-in-law. "There might have been a storm-cloud moment. And really, it isn't fair to these people. No one likes to be judged and I'm judging them for the people in my past."

"Church is hard, isn't it?" Grace said in sympathy. "It's the place where we should be loved, forgiven, nurtured. It's a place of mercy. But sometimes it isn't. We just have to remember that people are human and they bring all of their human frailties with them to church."

Sam hugged Grace, taking herself and her sister-in-law by surprise. "Thank you."

"You're welcome."

Brody had been busy buckling Bria into the back of the truck and he returned, glancing at his watch as he did. "Ready to go, ladies?"

"Yes, I'll meet you there. I'm going to stop by my place, and then head over to Jake and Breezy's."

"You're not backing out on us?" Brody questioned.

"I'm not backing out. But I am going to get my work clothes because I'll have to leave directly from there."

"Thirty minutes and I'm coming after you," Brody warned as he pulled keys from his pocket.

She kissed his cheek. "You know you're my favorite, right?"

"I'm everyone's favorite."

She kept her word. Not just because she knew Brody would come get her if she tried to skip out, but because she wanted a big family lunch. She wanted to spend time with her little nieces and the nephew Duke and Oregon had brought into the family. She wanted to hear more about the two children they were hoping to adopt in the near future.

As she parked in Jake's driveway, another truck pulled up. One she recognized immediately. Remington nodded his head as he got out. He reached into the back of the truck and pulled out a wheelchair.

She got out of her truck and watched as he lifted Parker from the back of the truck and situated the boy in his chair. Lee got out next. Gus was getting out on the front passenger side, pulling on his bent-up hat as he did.

"Samantha, guess what!"

"What?" she asked as Parker headed her way.

She glanced from the boy to Remington, who was coming up behind him, giving him a push to get on the sidewalk. It was a mistake, that look in his direction. He made a girl feel the need to go right back to church and pray against temptation. He was all cowboyed up in jeans that hung easy on his hips, boots and a button-up shirt with the sleeves rolled up, exposing darkly tanned forearms. She raised her gaze to meet his and he winked.

"How're you doing, Sammy?" he asked as he helped Parker on his way up the sidewalk.

A growl is not an appropriate response to a greeting. She remembered Duke telling her that when she was five and they took her to church. So she smiled sweetly at Remington and she didn't growl.

"I'm good, Remington." She squatted in front of Parker. "So, you told me to guess, but the only thing I can think of is that Remington really does have two heads—he just keeps one hidden inside his shirt!"

Parker laughed and laughed. Remington did a fake laugh. "Ha, ha."

"No," Parker finally said. "But he let me ride a horse."

"Ride a horse!" She shot Remington a look.

"He's nine and he loves to ride a horse."

"I rode in front of him and he even had special cuffs made for my legs since he's using the stirrups," Parker said joyfully.

"Well, that sounds like a lot of fun." She swallowed all of the reasons why it was a bad idea. When a little boy looked this happy, an adult didn't need to ruin it. Not in front of him.

"It was fun. We rode all over the place."

She ruffled her fingers through his dark hair. "You're my favorite cowboy, Parker. Now what do you say we head on in and see what Breezy has cooked up."

"I hope she has some of Duke's chocolate cream pie in there," Gus said as he joined them, walking a little slower than he had a few weeks ago. "I'm about ready to sit down with coffee and pie. Forget all the stuff that's good for us."

"Gus," his sister warned. "Be a good influence."

"Too late for that," Gus muttered. "I've been a bad influence most of my life, and I don't know how to change that any more than I know how to start eating vegetables."

Together they all headed inside where Lilly met them. After a cheerful hello she took control of Parker, pushing him off in the direction of the family room. Gus and Lee departed without looking back.

Sam was left alone with Remington.

She started to walk away, but he caught hold of her arm.

"Are you okay?" Remington asked.

"Okay about what?"

"With us being here?"

"Of course," she answered, probably too quickly. "I'm glad you're here. And now, I want to join my family for a Sunday lunch."

She slipped her hand into the pocket of the scrubs she'd changed into at her place. "I brought you something."

She handed him a letter from Tennessee.

"Is this what I think it is?"

"Marlie just turned nine. They sent a letter and pictures."

He held the envelope in one hand and pulled her close with the other. "I'm sorry. You've had nine years of doing this alone. I should have been there."

Yes, he should have been. But she couldn't say that. She couldn't drop accusations when it hadn't really been his fault that he hadn't known.

"I'm fine, Rem. As I get older, the letters get easier

to read. She's a funny girl with a big heart. She loves horses and art. They included a drawing to us from her."

"Why didn't you tell me you had this?" He looked hurt. He looked a little bit angry.

"I'm sorry, Rem. These letters are something I've done alone for so long."

"Yes, these letters and everything else. When will you begin to let people in? When will you realize it's okay to lean on someone?"

"I'm working on that. I am." She blinked against the sting of tears that his words had incited. "We should join them before they send someone looking for us."

"Yeah, of course. But later?"

Later. She knew what he meant. He wanted to talk. To delve further into the past and get things out in the open where they could examine each little detail of their lives. He was one of those people, the kind not willing to leave well enough alone.

Jake and Breezy's house was chaos. There were children running amok, adults arguing about baseball and who would win the bull-riding world finals come October. She stood in the living room for a minute, that room with its stone floors, wood walls and massive stone fireplace. She let her gaze travel from Jake, sitting on the edge of a chair watching bull riding, to Brody holding Bria and acting as if the sport had never been a part of his life. Gus sat in a nearby rocking chair making raspberry noises at the baby, playing peekaboo with her so that she laughed.

When Grace sat down next to Brody, Bria cried, reaching for her mommy. The twins, Rosie and Violet, were playing with dolls and appeared to be as sweet as two almost-preschool-aged girls could be. But Samantha knew about the secretive glances those little girls gave one another.

"This is your family," Remington said, his hand enclosing hers.

"Yes, they're something else." She slid her hand free. "I should go see if Breezy needs help in the kitchen."

"Running again?"

She shook her head. "No, not at all. I'm here, aren't I?"

His gray eyes captured her attention. Those eyes with the dark lashes and the faintest lines at the creases, evidence that time had gone by. Of course it had. And in the process they had changed, matured, maybe even come to their senses.

"You're still here," he repeated.

"I'm going now."

He laughed at the pronouncement. "Okay, head on to the kitchen like a good little woman."

"Oh, that was wrong. Duke is in the kitchen, too. Are you going to comment about his apron?" The mood lightened. Her heart felt a little freer.

"Not in a million years. Duke can bake, cook, wear an apron or a chef's hat, and I doubt anyone will tease him."

She kissed his cheek before walking away. It was a silly thing to do. Impulsive, really. A mistake? She wasn't sure. She left him standing in the living room wearing a stunned look. She hurried to the back of the house and the kitchen where she hoped she could forget for just a little while that Remington had a way of drawing her in and making her forget herself.

He was like driving reckless on a country road. Or racing her horse across the back field, taking no time to slow down for fallen logs and old fences. Loving him— yes, loving, because she did love him—was like closing her eyes and taking a leap without knowing what was ahead. And it scared her because it could either be wonderful, or leave her lost and alone.

In the kitchen Oregon was busy cutting up a salad. Breezy was putting whipped cream on a pie. Duke turned from his place at the stove. "About time you showed up. Can you put ice in glasses?"

Sam stepped into the kitchen to pull glasses from the cabinet. "Has anyone seen Parker and Lilly?"

"She took him to the family room to play a video game," Oregon answered as she diced tomatoes. "How's work?"

"Really good. Of course there are bad days, but there are a lot of good days, too."

"Bad days?" Duke asked, glancing back at her. "You haven't said much about that."

She shrugged off his observation. In the space of a heartbeat the conversation changed to the flea market in town and the new department store. Actually, the only department store in town. It was being built on an empty lot just down from Lefty Mueller's shop.

Oregon slid behind Duke, raising on tiptoe to kiss his shoulder as she moved on to help Breezy pull fresh-baked bread out of the oven.

Remington joined them, standing at the door of the already-crowded kitchen. For a crazy second Sam wished he would look at her the way Duke looked at Oregon, as if he would give her anything, do anything, to assure her happiness. If only she could trust someone enough to be that person for her.

Remington knew when to leave well enough alone. Most of the time. But when it came to Samantha, he forgot. Completely. At the strangest moments he would suddenly have an urge to be near her.

To prove that point, here he stood, risking her family's knowing looks. He'd been sitting in the living room with the guys. Parker had joined them, excited about a handheld game Lilly had taught him to play. But then Parker had gotten caught up in the PBR, forgetting Remington, forgetting the game.

Remington had headed for the kitchen. And Samantha.

"Anything I can do to help?"

"Help me fill glasses with ice." She pushed a couple of glasses at him. "If we get this show on the road, we can eat lunch before I have to go to work this afternoon."

He took the glasses and headed for the fridge. She followed.

Behind them Oregon and Duke were talking about more children. That led to talk about their house and the remodel that seemed unending. Couple talk. He glanced at Samantha. She moved him out of the way and held a glass under the spout for ice. He thought about having those conversations with her. But then his thoughts shifted, to the daughter they would have shared.

He hadn't allowed himself to think much about that little girl who would be about the same age as Parker. She was probably too young to really give them much thought. But someday she'd wonder about her parents. Who they'd been and why they'd given her up.

"Remington." Samantha's voice was soft, as if she knew where his thoughts had gone.

"Hmm?" He held glasses filled with ice and wondered where to put them. She set them on the counter.

"It's strange, isn't it? To be here. To have all of this family around us."

"We could leave?" he suggested, half teasing and half serious.

"I don't think we'd get away with that."

"Get away with what?" Duke's voice boomed from behind Remington.

Samantha chuckled a little and walked away, leaving him to face her brother.

"I guess I wasn't talking to you," Remington said.

"No, I guess you were talking to my little sister." Duke grinned. "Calm down, Jenkins. I'm teasing."

Oregon pulled on Duke's arm. "Stop."

Duke held up his hands, surrendering to his wife. "Can't anyone take a joke anymore?"

Some things didn't classify as a joke, Remington thought. When he thought about Sam, about the past, he didn't feel like joking.

He met her gaze from across the big kitchen and got tangled up in emotions from their past. These new feelings were something more, something lasting. Unless, of course, he was all alone in the feelings.

There were moments when he thought they were going in the right direction. And there were other moments when he knew for sure that she was pushing him away.

She joined him at the counter, setting down two more glasses that had been filled with ice. She handed him a pitcher of tea.

"You can fill," she said.

"I can do that." He took the pitcher and began pouring. "I read the letter. I was going to wait until later, but I couldn't resist."

She lowered her gaze. "I'm always the same way. I rip those letters open like it's Christmas morning. It's always a relief to know that she's okay. She's still a happy little girl with two parents that love her. Each year I look at the pictures and study her face, to make sure the look in her eyes matches what they tell me. I feel as if I would know if she wasn't really happy."

"I think she's really happy."

"Me, too."

He put his hand on hers, to stop her from moving away. "I'm glad you shared it with me."

She nodded but didn't look up, didn't meet his gaze. "I am, too. It's something I've always done alone."

"But you're not alone," he said.

"No, I'm not. For a long time it felt that way. Having the letters made me feel connected to her. As if in some small way I was a part of her life."

"You gave her life. There's nothing more important than that." He put the tea pitcher aside. "But Sam, when I say you're not alone, I mean because I'm here."

"I know you are."

He studied her face, wondering if she meant those words. Or if it was her way of getting out from under a conversation that was going too far.

For a moment he considered letting her off the hook, but he didn't.

"Sam, I'm not going anywhere. Ten years ago I let you down. That isn't going to happen a second time."

She took a step back and shook her head just the slightest bit. "This isn't the time."

No, maybe it wasn't. But eventually there would be a time. At seventeen he hadn't been the man she needed. Neither of them had been ready for a lifetime commitment.

Today was a different story. He couldn't imagine his life without her.

Chapter Fifteen

Samantha had worked three twelve-hour shifts in a row. When she woke up Wednesday morning she was ready for her day off. And she had the entire day planned. She was going to work with her horse, Buzz, paint her kitchen, then go to town for dinner at Duke's.

She started her morning with Buzz. After she'd worked him, brushed him down and put him back in the field, she cleaned the stall that Lady and her puppies claimed as their home. She watched as the puppies played in the yard with their mama. They were getting too big to keep confined to the stall and they loved the grass, chasing butterflies and tracking whatever scents they could find.

The smallest of the puppies, a little girl Sam had named Polly, lifted her hound dog nose and howled as if she'd managed to track something and had it treed in a nearby bush. In the distance Sam heard a car speeding up the long driveway. She shooed the puppies back toward the barn, not wanting to chance any of them getting under tires.

A familiar red convertible pulled to a quick stop in

front of the house. Kayla. She stepped out of the car, her dark hair pulled back with a scarf, big sunglasses covering her eyes.

Sam felt a mixture of emotions when she saw her half sister that they'd only come to know in the past year. Kayla was reckless, unhappy, and yet she cared about all of them. She cared about their mother, mess that she was.

"Kayla, where in the world have you been?" Sam called out as she headed across the yard.

Kayla smiled big, but it wasn't genuine. It was a mixture of sadness and desperation.

"I've been around. I just thought…" Kayla looked away, pulling off the sunglasses. "I thought I could stay here for a little while. I thought you might like to drive to Dallas with me."

"That's a lot of thinking," Sam said. She studied her sister, saw the weariness in her expression, the dark circles under her gray eyes. She was only twenty-three, but she looked older. "Are you okay?"

Kayla shook her head. "No, I don't think I am. But I'll be okay. I just need a place to stay for a while. I need to get my head on straight."

"You need to stop drinking," Sam said gently, not wanting to hurt the younger woman.

Kayla shook her head and started for her car. "This was a mistake."

"No, it wasn't." Sam went after her, grabbing her arm and stopping her from getting in the car. "I'm not going to judge you or lecture you. You can stay here as long as you want."

Kayla's hand was on the door of her car. She stood there, her back to Sam. "You don't mind?"

"I don't mind. Let's make a deal. I won't lecture you and you don't try to talk me into seeing her."

Kayla turned around, her bright, reckless smile back in place. "Deal."

They were more alike than Sam had ever realized. They were both a little bit lost, a little bit alone. But they were sisters. They didn't have to be lonely. They had each other.

"Cute puppies." Kayla inclined her head in the direction of the barn.

"Yes, and it won't be long before they have to find new homes."

"I'll take one," Kayla said softly, as if the thought of a dog was something she'd never considered.

"Of course." Sam glanced at her watch. "Let's go inside. I need something cold to drink. Have you eaten?"

Because it didn't appear Kayla had eaten in days. She was thin, pale and listless.

"Yes, of course I have. I'm not hungry."

Sam didn't lecture. Instead she led her sister through the front door of the house. A window air conditioner cooled the small room, the blinds closed to keep out the morning sun. The room was still bright and welcoming with overstuffed furniture, white end tables and aqua-blue walls. She wanted to paint the kitchen a sunny yellow to cover the light color that had started to fade and look dingy. She'd painted the cabinets when she first moved in. Little by little, she'd make this cottage her home.

Kayla followed her to the kitchen, restlessly pacing around that room as Sam poured them each a glass of iced tea. She found pie from the previous day and cut them each a slice.

"Duke's chocolate cream. Have a piece." She set it on the table with a fork.

"Thank you." Kayla sat down but didn't touch the pie.

"Kayla, I'm worried."

"No lectures, remember. I know you're worried. It's a strange thing, to have all of this family concern."

"I'm sure your dad is worried, too."

"Worried about his political career and worried people will find out about my mother. *Our* mother." Kayla picked up the fork and took a small bite of pie. "We won't pretend he really cares about me."

Because she didn't know Kayla's father, Sam didn't argue. She knew how it felt to believe a father didn't really care. They had lived strangely parallel lives without ever knowing the other existed.

The difference was that Sam had her brothers. Yes, they had been overprotective and made decisions she had fought against, but they'd loved her. She'd always had their love. Even when she'd felt desperately alone.

Kayla needed this family. She needed Sam, Brody, Jake and Duke. She needed their wives and their children.

She needed Martin's Crossing.

But Sam doubted she'd stay long. Kayla loved the city. She got restless, as if seeking something she couldn't find.

Faith. Sam could see it in her life, even though she'd danced around it for years. She could see it in the lives of her brothers, in the lives of her friends in Martin's Crossing. She saw the lack of faith in Kayla.

"Is that paint?" Kayla pointed with the fork.

"Yes, I'm going to paint my kitchen."

"By yourself?" Kayla looked truly astounded. "I'm impressed."

"Don't be. I'm not that good. You can help if you want."

Kayla lifted a shoulder in a careless shrug. "Sure."

Thirty minutes later the two of them were laughing together as they painted the first wall. Kayla definitely had no skill with a paintbrush. She had paint splattered on her face, on her hands and her clothes. She'd been telling Sam stories of her life in Austin and things she'd done to her father, just to embarrass him.

The stories were funny, and yet sad. Sam had been a daredevil most of her life, but in the past few years she'd stopped trying to get her brothers' attention. She'd settled in to college and career plans because she'd wanted to take control of her life.

Kayla controlled her life by creating headlines.

After another thirty minutes of painting, Kayla's expression turned serious. She focused on the section of wall she was painting, her bottom lip held between her teeth.

"She isn't all bad," Kayla said with a quick glance at Sam. "Oh, I know she did horrible things. But sometimes when I go visit her, she's kind. She seems to understand that I…" She hesitated. "She says she's there for me if I need her."

Their mother. Of course Kayla would go back to that subject. Sam kept painting, taking cautious strokes around the window. She could see Buzz grazing, and in the distance cattle moved to a new patch of grass.

"I'm glad she's there for you." Sam dipped the paintbrush in the can of paint labeled Goldenrod. "I used to dream that she'd come back and she'd be sorry for leaving. In my dreams she forced my dad to stop drinking. She brushed my hair each morning. She listened to me when I wanted to talk about my day at school. She read to me at night."

"I had the same dreams," Kayla admitted.

"We're a pair, aren't we?" Sam said. "But I understand why you take care of her and why you visit."

"Because I'm still a little girl waiting for her to come back and be who I need her to be," Kayla finished. "I blackmail my dad for the money to pay for the home she's in. He didn't want to do it, but he also doesn't want the world to know about her."

Sam didn't know what to say to that. She didn't get a chance to reply because Lady started barking. Then she heard a car door slam. Kayla looked a little worried.

"Probably one of our brothers," Sam assured her. She put her paintbrush down on the lid of the can, wiped her hands on a rag with some paint remover.

Someone knocked on the front door. Sam glanced out the window over the sink and saw Remington's truck parked next to Kayla's car. He knocked again on the front door. When she opened the door, she frowned at the man on her front stoop, a basket in his hands.

She opened the wood door but kept the storm door between them.

"No," she said.

He grinned. "Yes. We have some days to make up for. You've been at work and I've been moving cattle and taking some to the livestock auction."

"Days to make up for?"

He cocked his head to the side. "Don't pretend you've forgotten the plan."

"Stop being ridiculous." She still didn't open the door but it was hard to hide the smile trying to force its way to her lips.

Kayla walked up behind her and made an appreciative sound. "If you're turning him down, I'll take your place."

"No, you're not."

"Jealousy? Interesting." Kayla reached past her and pushed open the storm door. "Come on in, cowboy, and let me get you an iced tea."

Remington stepped inside, his gaze following Kayla from the room. "That would be the missing sister?"

"The one and only," Sam blocked him from watching, even though there was only curiosity in his gaze.

"Will she mind if you go with me?"

"We're not going anywhere."

"Oh, but we are." He opened the top of the basket. "I've got fried chicken, potato salad and chocolate cream pie."

"That's from Duke's. Don't tell me you have my own brother plotting against me."

"He's not plotting, darlin', he's *helping.*" He winked and managed to be ever so charming. "I've been assured this lunch is the way to a woman's heart."

"Rem," she started, but Kayla returned.

"I'm good if the two of you want to spend time alone. I can finish painting." Kayla plopped down on the sofa and grabbed a magazine. "Or sit here and read."

"There you go—no need to worry that you're leaving your company unattended."

No need to worry about her company, he said. But she had to worry about losing herself. She might have accepted with no qualms had she not been standing in this little house she'd worked so hard to make her own in the past couple of months. Her own place. Her own life.

"Don't overthink," Remington warned, as if he

knew where her thoughts were headed. But of course he didn't.

"Go," Kayla ordered from the sofa without looking up from her magazine.

Remington stood there, waiting for her answer. Waiting to see if she'd give in. Because it only took twenty-one days to develop a new habit. And maybe, just maybe, Remington was a little too close to making good on that. Because when a day or two went by and she didn't see him, she missed him.

"Okay," she conceded. "A picnic. Because it's already ninety degrees out there. And what's better than a picnic on a sweltering June day?"

She reached for a card that she'd left on the coffee table.

"Have a little faith, Sam." He took her by the arm and led her out to his truck.

"Where are we going?"

He opened the truck door for her. "Be patient and trust me."

Yes, patience. And trust. Two character traits she still needed to work on.

Remington got out of his truck and opened the gate just down from Duke's house. He headed back to the truck, but Sam had moved behind the wheel and drove the truck through the opening, then waited for him to close the gate and get back behind the wheel. She stayed in the middle of the seat, her shoulder close to his.

It felt like taking a step back in time, the two of them side by side in the cab of a truck. He took a well-worn trail through the field and headed to the hills and the creek. Country music played on the radio, songs about a girl and a boy falling in love. A small town. A pickup truck.

Ten minutes of driving led them to their destination, a creek at the base of a tree-covered hill. He backed the truck into a clearing and stopped.

"Here we are," he announced as he opened the door.

Sam slid out after him. "You definitely had this planned."

"Yep."

He put down the tailgate of the truck and hauled the basket out of the front floorboard. Sam walked to the edge of the creek and lifted her hair to pull it back in a ponytail. Her back was to him and he looked his fill, not at all upset when she caught him staring.

Her cheeks turned rosy pink and she looked away. "You know you're making this difficult, right?"

"I'm not trying to," he answered, searching for the right words. "I'm just doing my best to convince you to give us a chance."

"I'm giving us a chance."

"Then why are you still building walls between us?" He hadn't meant to go there, but he couldn't help it. He had a romantic picnic lunch, a perfect location on a perfect summer day. Why not tread into dangerous waters?

"I'm not building walls. I'm being cautious." She sat down on the edge of the tailgate and reached for a piece of chicken. "I…I'm afraid, Rem. Because we started like this once before, you and me."

"Yeah, we made mistakes. And we ended up going in different directions. But now we're here again. I can't help but think we're supposed to be here. Together."

"Faith," she sighed.

"Yes, Sam, faith. I'm not ashamed to be a man of

faith. I never expected this to be my path. I had a great government job and a nice place in Austin. But here I am, back in Martin's Crossing, running my granddad's ranch and pastoring a church. I wouldn't give it up for anything. And I'm not going to apologize for it."

"I didn't ask you to. I'm amazed by you. And when I compare myself, I come up short."

He leaned across the basket and touched his lips to hers. It was a sweet, simple kiss and he had a difficult time leaving it that way. With a sigh, he pulled away. "We could talk this to death, or we could just enjoy each other's company."

She nodded, picking up her plate and filling it with food, letting go a lot easier than he would have guessed. He held a plate full of food and scooted next to her. They sat on the tailgate, feet dangling, plates balanced on their laps. Sunlight filtered through the thick canopy of leaves. A light breeze cooled the air.

He could get used to days like this. And to Sam in his life.

"We're having a potluck at church tonight," he said.

"I told you, I don't bake casseroles." She didn't look at him, but he saw her mouth tilt upward.

"Well, then, we'll have to get you a cookbook," he teased. "But this doesn't require that you bake a casserole. I thought you might like to go with me."

For a long time she didn't answer. She focused on the chocolate pie on her plate for a while, then stared at the creek. Eventually she shook her head.

"I don't know if that's a good idea."

"Why not?"

One shoulder lifted and she took another bite of pie. "People will get ideas."

"They already have them, Sam. It isn't as if either of us are strangers to this community. They know us. They know our secrets. Not that we have any."

"Right, they all know. You're the pastor and I'm the woman who you sinned with."

He sat back and gave her a long look. "That came out of nowhere."

"No, it didn't. Like it or not, that's what we have between us. The elephant in the room is a child who turned nine last month."

What could he say to that? He could be angry. But he couldn't change anything. He'd heard that a person's present is their future. That long-ago summer had followed them both, changing them both in different ways.

The woman sitting next to him had built up walls and closed people out. She was still shutting him out of her life. But he'd meant what he said; he wouldn't walk away from his ministry.

For him it was all or nothing. He wanted her to be a part of it all.

"I'd like to not live in the past," he ventured with some caution.

"The past is always with us. It shapes us."

"Yes, it shapes us. It doesn't have to hold us prisoner."

"I wish that was true," she said softly. "I get a letter a few times each year, like a calling card from the past."

He reached for her hand because he didn't want to lose her with these words. "Sam, she's a happy little girl with a family that loves her. That's what those letters tell me. You did a great thing. It wasn't what you wanted. It wasn't the way we would have planned. But it happened and somehow God used it for good."

"No, it wasn't what I wanted." She pinched the bridge of her nose to stop the tears that threatened to fall. "I've gone to counseling. I've told myself she's better off. I've patted myself on the back and said what a good thing I've done. I've resented you for walking away without a scratch."

"Is that how you saw me? The guy who walked away without looking back?"

She didn't respond.

"I had scars, Sam," he assured her. "Some were from losing you. One your brother Brody gave me when he tossed me up against the barn wall. I still have that one if you want to see. I think I hit a nail."

A short burst of watery laughter. "Stop."

"Because you're starting to feel better and how terrible would that be?"

"I'm not sure yet." She finally looked at him. She had a dot of chocolate on the corner of her mouth.

"I'm sorry."

She nodded, then leaned into his shoulder. "Me, too."

He drew closer to her, but before he could taste that sweet corner of her mouth, she licked away the pudding. He grinned and kissed her anyway, tasting the remnant of the chocolate on her lips, loving her on so many levels it was frightening.

He loved her. And he worried they wouldn't find common ground. He didn't know if she would trust him in the hard times or keep pushing him away.

One thing he did know, a relationship couldn't work if both people weren't willing to trust and lean on each other.

But he was going to try his best to get there. With her by his side.

Chapter Sixteen

The picnic with Rem had left Samantha more uncertain than she'd ever been about anything. The uncertainty came from knowing that eventually she'd have to make a decision about her relationship with Remington. Because that's what it had become. Somehow over the past few weeks, he had managed to create a relationship between them that she hadn't expected.

It shouldn't have taken her by surprise. After all, he was the only one who had ever made her feel this way. With each touch, each word, each kiss, she fell further.

It wasn't as if she hadn't dated anyone since Remington. She had. But she'd always managed to hold herself back. She'd kept her heart intact because she'd been unwilling to allow anyone close enough to hurt her or to let her down.

She was cleaning up after a last-ditch attempt to get some painting done in her kitchen when Kayla appeared in her bathroom door, cell phone in hand. Sam met her reflection in the mirror.

"What's wrong?"

"It's our mom. It's Sylvia. She's had a heart attack." The air felt heavy, hard to breathe and static. "Okay."

Kayla pulled the phone from her ear. "I have to go. But I don't want to go alone."

"Brody will go with you."

Kayla shook her head. "I want you, Sam. I know it's selfish. But I want you to go with me. I want my sister."

"I'm not sure if I can." She faced her sister. "Kayla, I just don't know. I mean, I guess I can go. I don't want to see her but I can be there for you."

"That's all I'm asking."

Just then, her cell phone rang. Sam hurried to the kitchen to answer. The cell phone vibrated across the counter. She reached for it, glancing at the caller ID as she did.

"Rem," she answered. "Is everything okay?"

"Of course. I just wanted to give you one last chance to come to the potluck."

Suddenly a potluck sounded great. "I can't."

"It doesn't require a casserole. It doesn't require anything, really."

"I know."

"But you can't. Or won't?"

"I'm sorry," she said quietly, wishing she could tell him how much she needed him. She opened her mouth to explain, to ask him to come with her to Dallas.

"Sam, what's going on?"

She choked on emotion, holding it together as best she could. *Tell him*, her heart urged. *Let him in.*

"I have to make a trip to Dallas with Kayla."

"Do you need me to go with you?"

She closed her eyes and nodded. But she answered, "No, I've got this."

"Sam, let me come with you. Make room in your life for me. For us."

"I'm trying, Rem. This is me trying."

"Still afraid I'll let you down?"

"Old habits are hard to break."

"Yes, but there's that new habit we're working on, right?"

"We can't change everything with a few days spent together."

"Fine. Call if you need me," he said. But it sounded like a question.

She did need him, but she didn't tell him. Instead she hung up and told herself she could do this. She and Kayla could do this together.

She plugged her phone in to the charger and watched as Kayla poured a diet cola over ice and sucked it down.

"That's not good for you," Sam warned.

"I know, but I need caffeine or I'll go crazy. Do you want to drive?"

"I'd prefer it." If she didn't drive, she'd be forced to think about Remington, about the way he'd sounded hurt. About how much she wanted to let down her guard and let him take up residence in her heart and her life, nothing held back.

A few hours later she and Kayla were driving through Dallas. The city lights lent a glow to the dark nighttime sky. Traffic still buzzed along the main highways. Sam rolled down the windows and let fresh, humid air blow through the cab of the truck. In the passenger seat Kayla remained silent.

"You okay?"

Kayla startled and then nodded. "I'm good. We take the next exit."

"Got it." Sam continued to drive, trying not to think about Sylvia, about memories that her brothers had given her about the day their mother left. She'd heard the stories so many times she could picture it. But she'd been little more than a baby at the time. She'd been a toddler clinging to Jake and his twin, Elizabeth. Brody had screamed and cried, trying to go after her as she drove away.

Following the GPS directions, she pulled into the hospital parking lot. "Here we are."

"Yes," Kayla agreed, her tone flat. "I'm not sure why I've continued this relationship. Maybe because I worried that I'd be like her and I wanted to believe someone would be there for me."

"You're not like her."

Kayla got out of the truck. "How do you know?"

"From what my brothers have said, she was always this way. She didn't live thirtysome years normal and suddenly wake up unstable. She was this way even when Jake and Elizabeth were babies. Aunt Mavis said that our mother was always a little off, even as a child. She had problems, Kayla. I guess if she'd gotten help, taken medication, she might have been better. But she might not have."

Kayla preceded her through the sliding doors. "Sometimes it's difficult not to question my own sanity."

"I understand. But *you're* not her. *I'm* not her."

In the past, Sam had asked the same questions about herself, though. What if she was like her mother? What if she got married, had children and fell apart someday?

No, she wasn't Sylvia Martin. She wouldn't become Sylvia. Neither would Kayla. They got off the elevator and walked down a tile-floored hallway with bright fluorescent lighting. At room 205 they stopped.

"This is it," Kayla announced. She stood in front of the door, her hand poised to push it open.

Sam wrapped an arm around Kayla's shoulders and led her into the room. For her sister she could be the strong one. It also gave her the chance to be the detached one. She was here for Kayla. End of story.

But in a heart-stopping moment, her detachment ended. The second she looked at the woman in the hospital bed, her dark hair turning gray, her eyes hard and angry, everything changed. This pinched and drawn woman was her mother.

This was the woman who had left her little girls behind. Not because she didn't love them. Sam repeated words a therapist had once shared with her, that Sylvia might have left because she loved her children and hadn't wanted to hurt them anymore. Sylvia had loved them to the best of her ability.

That softened the reality and let Sylvia Martin off the hook. Samantha had never been in a place where she wanted to let this woman off the hook. Her own pain had been too raw, too deep. She'd needed to blame someone. That was the person who had left her alone.

"Kayla." Sylvia reached for Kayla's hand. "Look at you, losing weight."

"Look at you, in the hospital. How are you feeling?"

"I'm not good. They think I'm having a baby."

Dementia or psychosis? Sylvia had self-medicated with hard drugs, leaving her with brain damage. Sam's brothers had kept her updated on their mother's condition, whether she wanted the updates or not. Kayla shuddered and Samantha put a hand on her arm to offer her strength. "Mom, I brought Sam."

"Sam?" Sylvia shook her head, but the effort cost her and she laid back on the pillow. "I don't know Sam."

Sam told herself it didn't matter. So what if Sylvia didn't remember her? She'd forgotten Sam long before her memory started to fade.

Kayla took the seat next to their mother's bed. "Samantha is your daughter. She was your baby before me."

Sylvia reached for Kayla's hand. And there it was, the bond that Sylvia had with this one child. She'd left Kayla behind, too, but Kayla had sought her out and forced her to reciprocate in a relationship.

"Sam," Sylvia whispered and she looked past Kayla to Samantha. "You were a terror."

Sam laughed a little and it helped. It shook things loose inside her. She wiped at her eyes because she didn't want the tears to fall. "Yes. I was a terror."

The little girl in Sam waited for her mother to say more, to apologize, to tell her she loved her and was sorry she had to leave. Sylvia never said those words. She didn't say anything. She closed her eyes and slept with Kayla holding her hand.

Sam slipped out of the room. She found a vending machine and bought snacks and bottled water for herself and Kayla. When she returned, Kayla was still holding Sylvia's hand, still talking to her as if she heard. She told Sylvia about the grandchildren she had in Martin's Crossing. She told her about Duke's No Bar and Grill. She didn't mention her own life, her family, and Sam found that troubling.

After depositing the snacks on the table next to the bed, Sam picked up a second chair and moved it close to her sister. She handed Kayla a bottle of water and pushed the snacks toward her.

"Eat," she ordered.

Kayla picked a candy bar. "I used to dream that she'd come back to Austin, that she'd be the perfect mom and that my dad would suddenly be in love with her. We'd start a new family, the three of us."

"I'm sorry."

Kayla gave her a sharp look. "It's your story, too, Sam. You aren't removed from this."

Sam grabbed a bag of chips and opened them. She was far from removed. Instead she thought of her story, Kayla's story and another little girl who would someday wonder where her own mother was. Would her little girl dream up stories of a perfect mom, a perfect dad and imagine how they would rescue her?

She shook her head. No, her daughter was happy. Marlie hadn't been abandoned; she'd been offered a family.

"Sam?" Kayla's hand settled on her arm. "Are you okay?"

"I'm fine." She managed what she hoped was a carefree look.

"Right, of course you are. You're always fine, aren't you?"

Yes, she was always fine.

Until she wasn't.

Remington's phone calls were going unanswered. He'd tried Thursday and Friday to reach Sam. No man wanted to admit he was starting to feel a little desperate. But when she didn't answer, didn't call back, that's how he felt.

At Duke's on Saturday morning he spotted Brody sitting with a few local guys. He sat down at their table. Brody kicked back in his chair and reached for the cup of coffee on the table in front of him.

"How's things at the Rocking J?" Brody asked as he set his cup back on the table. "I heard you brought in a few new horses to strengthen bloodlines of your herd."

"We bought a couple of mares and a new studhorse,"

Remington admitted. But it was the last thing he wanted to discuss. Might as well get it over with. "Got him over at Stephenville. He's out of First For Cash."

"Racing stock, nice." Brody put a hand over his cup when Ned tried to refill it. "I've got to get home. But thanks, Ned. You're the only reason I come into this place."

"That and free coffee," she quipped as she filled Remington's cup. "Do you want breakfast, Rem?"

"An egg and toast. Thanks, Ned."

"You boys are all so polite today. You'd think you were tiptoeing around a subject you're not man enough to tackle."

"Now, Ned, give the man a break. He's sweating bullets over there," Brody teased with a big grin over the rim of his cup.

"I'm not sweating. You asked about our new horse and I told you."

Ned patted his shoulder. "Don't let him get under your skin."

"No worries, Ned."

"What about this horse of yours," Boone Wilder asked. "What color?"

"Chestnut," Remington answered. "How's the new business going?"

"Decent. We've been getting a few jobs a month. Lucy is on a job now," he said, referring to Lucy Palermo, one of his partners.

"That's great, Boone. How's your folks?"

Boone's dad had suffered a serious heart attack while Boone had been in Afghanistan. The past few years had been pretty tough on the Wilder family.

"They're good. Staying strong and praying hard to keep the ranch."

"We'll add our prayers to theirs," Remington said.

Brody glanced at his watch and made to get up.

"Brody, about Sam…"

Brody settled back into his chair. "I wondered when we would get around to her. She's at work. Been there a few days, as far as I can tell. She's been calling, asking me to feed her animals."

"Why is she staying there?" Remington didn't really need to ask. He figured Sam was avoiding him, avoiding her feelings about her mom and avoiding the family that wanted to help her through it all.

Remington leaned back when Ned approached with his plate and to refill his coffee.

"Working overtime," Brody said with a shrug. "I guess they lost a nurse and Sam is taking her shifts until they can hire someone."

"How's Sylvia?" Remington asked.

Brody shook his head. "Coma. I doubt she'll come out of it. I guess she was conscious when Sam and Kayla got there, but during the night something happened. They're doing tests but they think she had a massive stroke."

"That's tough, Brody. I'm sorry."

"Thank you. I guess none of us are really sure how to feel. Right now my biggest concern is Sam. She does her own thing, always has. Most of the time that keeps her lonely." Brody stood and tossed money on the table. "Tell Ned that's for her, not for the coffee."

Brody left. Conversation around the table skipped from topic to topic. Cattle prices, the never-ending need for rain, a truck someone had for sale. Remington took part, but his mind drifted to Sam. After breakfast he tried to call her again. She still wasn't answering.

If she was going to send him packing, she could do it face-to-face.

Chapter Seventeen

On a typical day, Samantha could deal with surprises. Today wasn't one of those days. She stood back as Remington led John Wayne through the children's ward, taking the horse from room to room. Dr. Jackson had personally invited the cowboy and his horse. It was Saturday and the children needed to be entertained. They needed to be distracted. She agreed. But did it have to be Remington and John Wayne doing the entertaining?

She lurked, trying to stay out of his way. She couldn't quite make herself stop watching him, though. Even as she took a seat behind the nurse's desk to finish up some paperwork, she found her gaze searching him out. And he caught her staring. He was leading John into another room and happened to look her way just as she happened to look at him. He didn't smile.

"Parker is having the time of his life, being the big guy who went home but came back to see his friends," one of the other nurses said as she took a seat next to Sam and logged in to her computer.

"I'm glad he brought Parker. He's doing so well and

his confidence is contagious." Sam watched Parker zoom ahead of Remington.

"Is it?" Beth asked. "Because if anyone could use a boost, Samantha, it's you."

"I'm fine," she assured the other woman. "I'm just tired."

"Stop taking all of the extra shifts. There's a temp service we can call and nurses who would like the hours."

"I didn't mean to take hours from anyone else," Sam said. "I was just trying to stay busy."

"Honey, I know that. I'm just saying, we can find someone to take those extra shifts. And I know you want to be here Monday when Lizzy has her going-home party."

"The Duncans? Right?" Sam asked, remembering the family that had stopped by a few times in the past week, getting to know Lizzy and learning about her care and rehab. "I'm so glad they're the ones."

"It just goes to show you how God works, Sam. We were all upset when those other families turned our Lizzy down. But if they hadn't backed out, she wouldn't be going home with this family."

"Yes, it did work out for the best."

Sam pushed aside the file in front of her and signed out of her computer. "I'm going to check on Danny before I go home."

"You're actually going home?" Beth looked up from her computer. "That's good. Get some sunshine and fresh air."

Sam nodded and headed for Danny's room. She peeked in, a little bit afraid she'd find Remington and John Wayne at the boy's bedside. Instead she found Danny sitting on the edge of his bed, playing a game.

"Hey, kiddo, how are you feeling?"

Danny looked up from the game. "I beat level four. That's giant."

"I'm sure it is. Do you need anything before I go home?"

Danny shook his head. "Where's Parker?"

"He's somewhere out there. We told him to let you sleep. But now that you're awake I'll give him the all clear."

"Thanks!"

She found Parker in the hallway just leaving another room. "Parker, my friend."

Parker gave her a fist bump and a big grin. "Is he awake now?"

"He is awake. He's wondering what's taking you so long to get in there."

Parker laughed at that. "He didn't say that, you did. Guess what."

"What?"

Parker backed up and went forward. "I can do wheelies."

"Oh, great, that's exciting and terrifying."

Then he was gone, heading through the door with a shout. She heard Danny say something about his crutches. He'd tossed aside his prosthetic for now because it had caused some hot spots that made it hard to wear. As she eavesdropped, Danny told Parker about the new treatment and his move to Dallas that would happen at the end of the week. He made it sound like an adventure, leaving out the details of the treatment. He promised he'd call and write Parker, and when he was better, they'd get together.

She prayed it would all work out exactly the way Danny planned.

With her mind on the two boys, she didn't see Remington in front of her until it was too late. She came to a halt just short of bumping into John Wayne. The little horse snorted and shook his head.

"Oops, sorry. I was just…" Remington was standing in front of her, blue jeans, blue shirt and a cowboy hat pulled low. He reminded her of her favorite blanket, the one she loved to curl up with because it made her feel warm and secure. She shook her head at that thought.

"Avoiding me?" The corner of Remington's mouth kicked up.

"No, not avoiding you." Okay, she had been. But she had a reason to avoid him. She had many reasons.

"Sam, we need to talk."

"Rem, I don't want to talk."

"No, you want to push everyone away."

"Are you here to tell me you know how I feel?" She sighed and started to reach for him, but that would be too much. "I'm sorry, that wasn't fair."

"No, it wasn't. But I'm sure you've had a few people telling you how to feel and it makes sense that you're a little sensitive. I guess I'm here for more personal reasons. I've been trying to call and you're avoiding me."

Nervous, she licked her lips. "Yes, I know. I'm not sure what to say. I miss you. And missing you this much scares me."

"You wouldn't have to miss me if you'd answer the phone. Or if you'd let me come over and check on you."

"Check on me, why?"

He gave her a look. "Because seeing your mom after all of these years had to be tough."

"I'm fine. You really don't have to check on me."

He took a step back, still giving her that steady, careful gaze with gray eyes that seemed to see too much. She wanted to look away but didn't. She held his gaze, wanting him to see she was fine.

"Okay, I won't check on you. I'll leave you to your work."

"Rem," she called out to him.

"Sam, I'm not going to force my way into your life. I've been banging on the door, trying to make you see that I love you and I want to be a part of your life. But you're building up walls faster than I can knock them down."

"I'm not... I just..." He'd just said he loved her. She took a deep breath and met his gaze head-on. "I don't know how to be the person you want or need me to be. I don't bake casseroles. I'm not a pianist or a Sunday school teacher."

"Are those the qualifications for a pastor's wife?" A glimmer of amusement settled in his eyes. The look quickly faded back to serious.

"The ones I can think of right now."

He pulled the small horse close to his side. "I guess I didn't get that list. Because what I'm looking for is someone who will be my partner. A woman who trusts me enough to call me when she needs someone. A woman who wants me by her side when she goes through hard times. And I want that same woman to be that person for me."

He walked away, leaving her standing there in the hall, wondering how she'd recover from an *I love you* and what sounded like goodbye.

She knew that Remington meant what he said. He loved her. And she loved him. It was all of the stuff in between that threatened their happiness.

What frightened her the most was the part about being who he needed her to be. Because if she couldn't be that person, and he walked away, what would be left of her?

* * *

The ride back to Martin's Crossing from the Braswell hospital didn't take long. With Parker talking nonstop about Danny, and about Lizzy's going-home party, it felt even shorter. The kid had a lot to say about their visit at the hospital.

"So, why are you and Sam fighting?" Parker asked as they drove up to the barn at the Rocking J.

"Why do you think we're fighting?"

"Because I saw the two of you. I'm almost ten, you know."

"Yeah, I know. That makes you a relationship expert?" Remington eased on the brake to keep John Wayne from getting jolted too badly.

"Yeah, kind of." Parker grinned and laughed a little. "Gus said you've got it worse than any lovesick kid he's ever seen."

"I'm not a kid. I'm a grown man."

"With a crush. That's what Aunt Lee called it."

"It isn't a crush." And then he shook his head. "I'm not having this conversation with you."

"Sometimes we have to face our feelings. That's what I learned in therapy. We can't hide it, because it's going to come out. And that's never good. At least that's what I think Dr. James said."

Remington sighed as he got out of the truck and walked around to the back to retrieve Parker's wheelchair.

"Have you told her how you feel?" Parker asked as he settled in his chair.

"Of course," he said. Hadn't he?

"Gus said never take it for granted that a woman knows how you feel. You'll end up in trouble." Parker looked up at him. "Women like gestures. That's what Gus said."

Remington grabbed the handles of the wheelchair and helped the boy maneuver over rough ground. "He told you that? Because you're having relationship troubles. At nine."

"Almost ten," Parker reminded. "And yes, he told me when we were talking about you and Sam."

"You're nine going on ninety. Head for the house, kid. I'm going to unload John and take care of the other livestock."

"I can help," Parker said, stopping his chair.

"I'd kind of like to be alone."

Parker gave the wheels a good push and glanced back over his shoulder as he headed for the house. His brown hair was messy and his eyes sparkled with amusement. "Okay. But if you need to talk…"

"I know where to find you." Remington smiled as he said it. How could he not smile at that kid?

Remington unloaded John Wayne. It wasn't much of a challenge. He opened the back of the trailer, the horse backed out and headed for the barn. When Remington got to the barn, John was already inside his stall, waiting at a bucket that he thought should hold feed.

"You're full of yourself, John."

At that, John rubbed his head on Remington's leg.

He gave the horse a scoop of grain, then checked his water bucket. John was munching on grain, letting oats drip from his mouth as he went for a drink of water. The water dribbled from his dark muzzle. Remington gave the horse a pat and walked away.

From his stall at the end of the barn, the new stallion let out a whinny that shook the rafters. Remington headed that way. The horse had his head out, waiting for attention. His ears were pricked forward and his luminous brown eyes were watching, taking in his new surroundings. He was young, but he had a lot of promise. Remington hoped he'd made the right choice. The horse had a good temperament, strong confirmation and the best bloodlines.

"Parker said you saw Samantha at the hospital," Gus said from behind him.

"Didn't see you come in." Remington patted the horse's neck and moved away from the stall. He knew his granddad would follow.

"I'm sneaky. How's she doing?"

"Good as can be expected."

"How are you doing?" Gus asked, his gray eyes squinty beneath silver brows that almost met in the center.

"Now I know where Parker gets it." He walked through the back door of the barn and to the fence, scanning the cattle that grazed. "Have you seen number 213?"

"Now that you mention it, no I haven't. She's probably gone off to have that calf."

"I didn't notice her this morning, either. I'll take a drive and see if I can find her."

"Her mama was about the worst cow in the world for needing a calf pulled. I'll go with you," Gus offered.

"I don't think you ought to," Remington countered.

And he meant it. His granddad had trouble walking on level ground. The last thing he needed was to fall and get hurt.

"I'm a grown man and I'll do what I want. Remington, I'm careful. But I'm not going to sit back in my rocking chair and stop working."

Remington let out a breath. "I know, Gus. I'm sorry."

"No, you're just all worked up, trying to figure out how to make things right with Sam. I guess the best thing you can do for that little girl is let her know you're going to be here for her when she needs you."

"I've done that. I've told her every way I know how that I'm here for her. And she doesn't seem to want that."

"Give her time," Gus said as he pulled himself into the truck.

Rem got behind the wheel and they took off through the field, both of them watching for a red hide hidden in tall grass or a stand of trees.

"How much time do I give her, Gus?" Remington hadn't meant to ask the question, but it slipped out and he couldn't take it back.

"I guess as long as she needs to work through whatever is holding her back."

"That could take a long time. What if *I'm* what's holding her back?"

"I reckon that might be part of it. She's been on her own for a bit."

"Yeah, I guess she has." Remington spotted the cow. "There's our cow. Looks like she's down."

"Hand me that cane in the back and I'll follow you. Do you want me to call the doc?"

"I don't see a reason why. She's got more important things to deal with than a downed cow. It's not like we haven't pulled a few calves in our time."

"Yeah, but I'm not much help these days."

"You're still good help." Remington headed toward the cow. "Bring the ropes."

"Got them," Gus called out. "Just think how nice it would be for you and Sam to run this ranch together."

"Stop," Remington called back to his granddad. "I'm not going to push my way into anyone's life, so you need to realize Sam and I are probably never going to be more than just friends."

Gus mumbled something under his breath that sounded like "if I leave it up to you, that's what I'm afraid will happen."

Remington didn't ask him to repeat what he'd said. He didn't really need to hear it. So far today he'd had advice from a nine-year-old and an almost-eighty-year-old. Advice wasn't going to change his feelings or Sam's heart.

He wasn't even sure if time was going to change things.

Chapter Eighteen

The day Sylvia Martin died was much like any other. Sam was at work when Brody showed up to give her the news. She didn't cry. She was numb. Too numb to know how she really felt about losing the woman who had never really been a mother to her.

Dr. Jackson told her to go home. He told her to take a few days to allow herself to grieve. Grief. She'd felt it before. When her brothers had sent Remington away. When they'd sent her away. And the greatest grief of all, when her daughter had been taken from her arms.

She couldn't allow herself to believe what she felt for Sylvia was grief. And yet...

When she walked through the front door of her little house, she found Kayla asleep on the sofa. Sam left her shoes on the mat and tiptoed through the room to the kitchen. Kayla had finished painting it.

The goldenrod-yellow color was a sunny contrast to the aqua blue of the living room. The paint job wasn't half-bad, either. There were a few drips and a couple of spots on the ceiling. She looked around, taking in the job her sister had done.

People could learn new skills. Or habits. She chuckled at the thought because it brought to mind an image of Remington, his smile, the amused flicker in his eyes as he teased her about becoming a habit in her life.

She opened the fridge to look for something to eat. Her stomach growled, reinforcing the thought that it was dinnertime. A sandwich, maybe a frozen dinner or a salad. She had canned soup in the cabinet.

What she wanted was a casserole. She wanted something with potatoes and beef and cream of something. But she didn't have a cookbook.

She pulled a can of soup out of the cabinet and found a recipe on the back. Perfect. Tater Tots, ground beef, cream of mushroom soup. She had the ingredients. She had the ability.

She could and would fix a casserole for dinner.

She was frying the beef in a skillet when Kayla wandered in, sleep still clouding her eyes. Her dark hair was pulled back in a messy bun.

"I didn't expect to see you on my sofa," Sam said.

"I hope you don't mind. I didn't know where else to go." Kayla looked away with the admission, tears filling her eyes.

This wasn't how it should be when a mother died. A family should be together. "Kayla, I'm sorry."

She reached for her sister and was surprised when Kayla stepped close, allowing the hug. The two embraced for a long time. When they pulled apart Sam brushed away the tears streaming down her cheeks. She grabbed a couple of paper towels and handed one to her sister.

"We're a mess," Sam said. She was the older sister. She hadn't thought about it before. Kayla needed her to say and do the right thing. She had to be the person who didn't sweep someone else's grief under the rug, as if it didn't matter.

"I know she wasn't much of a mom, but she was our mom. And I'm going to miss her."

"I know," Sam admitted. "I understand. I think I'm going to miss the idea of who she might have been."

"Maybe that's all we have?" Kayla blew her nose. "I don't mean to be a mess. I just wanted to be with someone who understands. I didn't want to go home to my dad. He asked me to come back to Austin."

"He loves you."

Kayla let out a long sigh. "I don't know. I'm not sure if its love or if he just wants me home to put on a show for him."

"Don't rush off, then. Stay here as long as you like."

Kayla started to make coffee. "Thanks. What are you making?"

"A casserole. It just seems like the right thing to do. I'm going to make a huge casserole and then call our family together. We should all be together."

"What about the funeral?"

Sam hadn't really thought that far ahead. "We have a family cemetery."

Kayla brushed a hand across her face. "I can't stop crying."

"I know."

Her phone rang. She glanced at the caller ID. It was Remington. She reached for it, but she didn't answer. She couldn't. Not yet. She needed to do something to fight the emptiness. She needed to bake a casserole. She needed to be with her family. For the first time, she wasn't going to be alone when the grief hit. She wasn't going to handle things alone because she had no one to turn to. She had a family.

The phone rang again. Remington.

"Answer it," Kayla pushed the phone into her hand.

She answered. "Hi, Remington."

"I heard the news. Are you okay?"

She didn't know how to answer that. At the moment she was doing what she did, handling things.

"I'm good."

"Of course you are. Sam, let me come over."

"I'm going to call my brothers ..." All at once, the grief became a living, breathing thing that took her by surprise. Tears streamed down her cheeks and she couldn't get the words past the lump in her throat.

Kayla took the phone from her and Sam slid to the floor, burying her face in her hands. Sylvia Martin would never come back to them. She wouldn't bake cookies or listen to her daughter pour out her heart when things got bad.

So many childhood dreams, lost.

Kayla settled on the floor next to her. The two of them held each other for a long time, crying tears for a woman who could never be who they needed her to be. After a while they brushed away their tears. Sam reached for her sister's hand and held it tight.

"The best thing she did was giving me a sister," Sam said as she stood, pulling Kayla to her feet. "And we're going to make that casserole."

Kayla laughed at that. "You make it sound like we're scaling Everest."

"Have you ever made one?"

"Not a good one. Haven't you?"

Sam shook her head. "No, I haven't."

Kayla leaned on the counter and watched as Sam put the ground beef in the pan. "I guess it's time to try new things."

New habits. Sam drew in a breath and nodded. She missed Remington. She missed him in a way that shook her. Because she'd been missing him for so long, she hadn't realized that this was a new kind of longing. This was the kind of need that went beyond a summer romance. Ten years ago she'd needed someone to make her feel safe, to feel loved. It had been a selfish thing, that summer love of theirs. She'd been so lost and hurt, and he'd been there.

Now she needed to love him back. But she'd pushed him away. More than once.

"Are you okay?" Kayla asked as she leaned against the counter watching Sam put the casserole together in the pan before sliding it into the oven.

"I'm good." Sam closed the oven door on a sigh. "I've really blown it with Rem."

"Yeah, maybe. Maybe not. Give it time, Sam. We'll get through one thing at a time and then the two of you can talk."

"Yes, maybe."

Headlights flashing through the window meant they had company. Sam headed for the living room in time to see another truck behind the first. Her brothers. All three of them and their families. Kayla leaned in behind her, watching the invasion of the Martins.

"This is what family is all about," Kayla said. "I like it."

Another flash of headlights came up the driveway. Remington's truck pulled up to the barn. She watched him get out, saw him stop to talk to Jake, and then look toward the house.

"I'll be back," she told Kayla as she pushed the screen door. "Oh, can you take the casserole out of the oven if I'm not back before the timer goes off?"

"You won't be back."

Breezy and Grace met her on the sidewalk, Brody behind them. Duke and Oregon were just getting out of their truck. Breezy pulled her close and hugged her. Then it was Grace's turn.

"Remington called," Breezy said. "We all thought we should be together."

"Yes, we should." Sam smiled at her sisters-in-law, then her attention refocused on the man walking next to her brother. "We'll have to make plans. I have a casserole in the oven."

Duke pulled her close and held her tight. "A casserole?"

She nodded into his shoulder. "It seemed like the right thing to do. At times like this, people make casseroles. They drink coffee and talk until late. They share stories."

"We don't have a lot of stories," Duke said.

"No, but we'll make some, won't we?" She stepped back, looking into his eyes, needing his reassurance.

"Yes, we'll make stories."

One by one her family tromped past her into the house. She could hear their voices, loud and raucous. She could hear the children laughing as adults played with them. Remington headed her way, a rectangular, brown-paper-wrapped package in his hands.

"You shouldn't have come, but I'm glad you did." She touched his arm, letting her hand linger for a minute.

"You've gone through too much alone, Sam. Even if you think her death doesn't matter to you, it does. She was your mom. She gave you life."

"Yes, she did." Tears burned her eyes and trickled down her cheeks. "I should go in. They're all in there."

"Yes, you should go." His hand reached out and brushed through her hair.

She closed her eyes at the tenderness of it. A dangerous, clawing need tugged at her heart. A need for him to hold her, to make her feel safe. It frightened her, that need for him, that need to be a part of his life.

But what frightened her more was the thought of not having him.

"I need to go inside," she repeated, smiling. "I baked a casserole."

"A casserole, huh?"

She nodded. "Yes, and I think I nailed it."

He grinned, and he slid an arm around her waist to pull her close. "I never doubted you."

"What's the package?" she asked, pointing at the box.

"A grand gesture," he said as he handed it to her.

"A grand gesture?"

"Yes. Parker said I need a grand gesture if I'm going to get anywhere with you. I took his advice."

"Maybe I should wait." She held the package, her heart trembling with uncertainty.

"No, I think you should open it. And I think you should know that I love you. I'm willing to wait. I'm willing to give you time and space. But I'm not willing to let you go."

They stood in the dark, just at the edge of the porch light's pale glow. Remington knew he would always remember this night. He prayed it would be a night they both remembered. He hoped it would be the night that changed everything for them. He hadn't really planned it this way. But here they stood and he knew, without a doubt, that he needed this woman in his life forever.

She looked up at him, her blue eyes glistening with unshed tears, her fingers trembling as she untied the string and removed the brown paper. She struggled with the box and he pulled out a pocketknife to slice the tape that held it closed.

"Thank you," she whispered.

She opened the box and pulled out the framed picture. Her sharp, indrawn breath revealed the moment she recognized the sketch in the frame. An awkward drawing of a horse, the ears and eyes large, the mane shaggy. In the corner the name *Marlie*, spelled in grade school penmanship.

She held it to her and tears trickled down her cheeks.

"Oh, Rem—" she shook her head "—it's beautiful, sweet and definitely a grand gesture."

"I'm glad you like it."

"Like it? I love it." She drew in a breath and let it out on a sigh. "Somewhere out there is a little girl with your hair and my eyes. And she's happy. She dreams of horses and someday marrying a prince. I think sometimes she thinks about us. But she's happy. And I know that what I did, as hard as it has been, was the right thing to do. I'm just sorry that I wasn't able to tell you. I'm sorry we didn't make the decision together."

"I'm sorry I wasn't there for you, Sam. But I'm here now. And I want to be here for you every single day for the rest of our lives."

"I'm a mess," she said, reaching to touch his cheek.

"I've got it on good authority you can bake a casserole."

"I think you should taste it before you make any decisions," she teased.

"I'm not worried about the casserole. I'm not worried that you can't play the piano or teach Sunday school. I just want to know that you'll be with me."

She moved close, the hand on his cheek touching his hair. He pulled her close and claimed her lips, claimed her heart as his. She was soft, sweet and everything he had ever needed.

When he stepped back she smiled up at him.

"What?" he asked, a little uncertain because of the humor that flashed in her blue eyes.

"You're a hard habit to break, Remington Jenkins. And I love you. I'm looking forward to our summer romance."

"And a fall wedding?"

She nodded and kissed him again. "Yes."

Epilogue

Sam held a bouquet of zinnias as she walked down the aisle to a George Strait song. She and Remington had decided this wedding would be theirs in every way. George Strait. Remington in dark jeans and a button-up shirt. Sam in a Western-styled wedding dress of white lace and pearls. They didn't have bridesmaids. No one walked her down the aisle. At the front of the church Remington stood with his best man, Parker. Lilly waited on the opposite side to stand with Sam.

Outside, Duke had arranged a barbecue that would feed the entire town for days.

But inside that church two lives were going to become one. It had taken them ten years and a few months to get here, to an autumn wedding and a life together.

Sam stopped at the front of the church and faced Remington. He winked and she reached for his hands. The pastor cleared his throat. She let go and waited for the cue.

Behind them people laughed a little. She heard someone crying. They were finally asked to take each other by the hand and repeat the vows to love one another, in sickness and in health, richer, poorer, through good times and bad.

They'd already been through some hard times. They'd shared some amazing times. They were sure to weather every storm with faith, knowing they could get through whatever came at them.

"I love you," she whispered as the pastor spoke about the ring symbolizing eternity.

And then they waited for a few awkward moments as Parker dug around in the seat of his wheelchair, searching for the rings. After a few heart-stopping moments he pulled them out of his pocket and said, "Ta-da!"

They laughed until they cried. The best kind of laughter.

Then they were husband and wife. Remington kissed his bride, holding her close.

"I'm going to love you forever, Mrs. Jenkins."

"I'm going to love you forever, Mr. Jenkins," Sam whispered in his ear. They kissed again, and then he took her hand and led her from the church.

As they hurried to the tent where the cake was set up, waiting for them, the band played a song about loving each other forever. Forever and ever, amen.

* * * * *

Keep reading for an exclusive excerpt of
THE RAIN SPARROW
by New York Times *bestselling author*
Linda Goodnight.
Available now from HQN Books!

Dear Reader,

Welcome back to Martin's Crossing! I'm so thrilled to be able to bring Samantha Martin's story to life. In the beginning, Sam was a bit of a mystery, even to me. She was sent away by older brothers who weren't quite sure what to do with a younger sister intent on getting herself into trouble. Now she's back home where she's determined to live her own life. Past and present collide and Sam has to deal with the man she thought never to see again.

I hope you enjoy Samantha and Remington's story!

Brenda Minton

A mystery writer and a shy librarian find love on a dark, stormy night in Honey Ridge, Tennessee...

BARE FEET SOUNDLESS on the cool tile flooring, Carrie moved to a pantry and removed one of Julia's sterling silver French press urns. "We'll have to grind the beans. Julia's a bit of a coffee snob."

"Won't the noise disturb the others?"

Thunder rattled the house. Carrie tilted her head toward the dark, rain-drenched window. "Will it matter?"

"Point taken. You're a lifesaver. What's your name?"

"Carrie Riley." She kept her hands busy and her eyes on the work. The fact that she was ever-so-slightly aware of the stranger with the poet's face in a womanly kind of way gave her a funny tingle. She seldom tingled, and she didn't flirt. She was no good at that kind of thing. Just ask her sisters. "Yours?"

"Hayden Winters."

"Nice to meet you, Hayden." She held up a canister of coffee beans. "Bold?"

"I can be."

She laughed, shocked to think this handsome man might actually be flirting a little. Even if she wasn't. "Bold, it is."

As she'd predicted, the storm noise covered the grinding sound and in fewer than ten minutes, the silver pot's lever was pressed and the coffee was poured. The dark, bold aroma filled the kitchen, a pleasing warmth against the rain-induced chill.

Hayden Winters offered her the first cup, a courteous gesture that made her like him, and then sipped his. "You know your way around a bold roast."

"Former Starbucks barista who loves coffee."

"A kindred spirit. I live on the stuff, especially when I'm working, which I should be doing."

She didn't want him to leave. Not because he was hot—which he was—but because she didn't want to be alone in the storm, and no one else was up. "You work at night?"

"Stormy nights are my favorite."

Which, in her book, meant he was a little off-center. "What do you do?"

He studied her for a moment and, with his expression a peculiar mix of amusement and malevolence, said quietly, matter-of-factly, "I kill people."

ELIJAH AND THE WIDOW
Lancaster County Weddings • by Rebecca Kertz

Hiring the Lapp family men to make repairs around her farmhouse, Martha King soon develops feelings for the younger Elijah Lapp. Now it's up to the handsome entrepreneur to show the lovely widow that age is no barrier for true love.

THE FIREFIGHTER DADDY • by Margaret Daley

Suddenly a dad to his two precocious nieces, firefighter Liam McGregory enlists hairdresser Sarah Blackburn for help. He's quickly head over heels for the caring beauty, but will the secret he keeps prevent them from becoming a family?

COMING HOME TO TEXAS
Blue Thorn Ranch • by Allie Pleiter

Returning to her childhood ranch, Ellie Buckton teams up with deputy sheriff Nash Larson to teach after-school classes to the town's troubled teens. Can she put her failed engagement in the past and find a future with the charming lawman?

HER SMALL-TOWN ROMANCE • by Jill Kemerer

Jade Emerson grew up believing Lake Endwell, Michigan, was a place where dreams come true. So why is Bryan Sheffield leaving? Can she convince the rugged bachelor to give his hometown—and love—a second chance?

FALLING FOR THE MILLIONAIRE
Village of Hope • by Merrillee Whren

When Hudson Conrick's construction company works on the women's shelter expansion at the Village of Hope, he'll prove to ministry director Melody Hammond that he's more than just an adventure-loving millionaire—he's her perfect match.

THE NANNY'S SECRET CHILD
Home to Dover • by Lorraine Beatty

Widower Gil Montgomery is clueless on how to connect with his adopted daughter—until he hires nanny Julie Bishop. He quickly notices she has a special way of reaching his little girl—and of claiming his heart.

LICNM0316

REQUEST YOUR FREE BOOKS!

2 FREE INSPIRATIONAL NOVELS
PLUS 2
FREE
MYSTERY GIFTS

YES! Please send me 2 FREE Love Inspired® novels and my 2 FREE mystery gifts (gifts are worth about $10). After receiving them, if I don't wish to receive any more books, I can return the shipping statement marked "cancel." If I don't cancel, I will receive 6 brand-new novels every month and be billed just $4.99 per book in the U.S. or $5.49 per book in Canada. That's a saving of at least 17% off the cover price. It's quite a bargain! Shipping and handling is just 50¢ per book in the U.S. and 75¢ per book in Canada.* I understand that accepting the 2 free books and gifts places me under no obligation to buy anything. I can always return a shipment and cancel at any time. Even if I never buy another book, the two free books and gifts are mine to keep forever.

105/305 IDN GH5P

Name _____ (PLEASE PRINT)

Address _____ Apt. #

City _____ State/Prov. _____ Zip/Postal Code

Signature (if under 18, a parent or guardian must sign)

Mail to the **Reader Service:**
IN U.S.A.: P.O. Box 1867, Buffalo, NY 14240-1867
IN CANADA: P.O. Box 609, Fort Erie, Ontario L2A 5X3

**Are you a subscriber to Love Inspired® books
and want to receive the larger-print edition?
Call 1-800-873-8635 or visit www.ReaderService.com.**

* Terms and prices subject to change without notice. Prices do not include applicable taxes. Sales tax applicable in N.Y. Canadian residents will be charged applicable taxes. Offer not valid in Quebec. This offer is limited to one order per household. Not valid for current subscribers to Love Inspired books. All orders subject to credit approval. Credit or debit balances in a customer's account(s) may be offset by any other outstanding balance owed by or to the customer. Please allow 4 to 6 weeks for delivery. Offer available while quantities last.

Your Privacy—The Reader Service is committed to protecting your privacy. Our Privacy Policy is available online at www.ReaderService.com or upon request from the Reader Service.

We make a portion of our mailing list available to reputable third parties that offer products we believe may interest you. If you prefer that we not exchange your name with third parties, or if you wish to clarify or modify your communication preferences, please visit us at www.ReaderService.com/consumerchoice or write to us at Reader Service Preference Service, P.O. Box 9062, Buffalo, NY 14240-9062. Include your complete name and address.

LII5